# Lot's Daughters,
## Ancestors of King David

# Lot's Daughters,
## Ancestors of King David

Carole Lunde

# LOT'S DAUGHTERS, ANCESTORS OF KING DAVID

Scripture quotations marked RSV are taken from the Revised Standard Version of the Bible, copyright © 1946, 1952, 1971 by the Division of Christian Education of the National Council of the Churches of Christ in the USA. Used by permission.

iUniverse books may be ordered through booksellers or by contacting:

iUniverse
1663 Liberty Drive
Bloomington, IN 47403
www.iuniverse.com
1-800-Authors (1-800-288-4677)

ISBN: 978-1-5320-8695-3 (sc)
ISBN: 978-1-5320-8696-0 (e)

Print information available on the last page.

iUniverse rev. date:  10/31/2019

# CONTENTS

# CHAPTER 1

≈≈≈≈≈≈≈≈≈≈≈≈≈≈≈≈≈≈≈≈≈≈≈≈≈≈≈≈≈≈≈≈≈≈≈≈≈≈≈≈≈≈

# HARAN

Our story begins in biblical Haran, universally identified with Harran, a city whose ruins lie within present-day Turkey.

Haran was the place where Abram settled with his wife, Sarai, and his father, Terah. They had journeyed west from Ur to Haran, and then when God spoke to Abram, they went south into the Land of Canaan, now referred to as the Promised Land.

Abram lived in Haran until his father passed away before continuing his journey. When his father died, Sarai and Abram's nephew, Lot, accompanied him with people from Haran, servants of the family, and a newcomer to their family to the Promised Land.

Abram was an imposing man with a full head of auburn hair and bushy beard. He commanded respect wherever he went. Word was that his family ancestry was royal. No one knew for sure. Abram never spoke of his family, but his demeanor spoke of a princely influence from somewhere in his background.

Sarai was tall and queenly. She was willowy and graceful which hid her innate strength and wisdom. Her hair was flaxen and flowing, a throwback to a relative from long ago in a far country. Together she and Abram were a striking couple that turned heads wherever they went.

Zehra was the eldest daughter in her family and not eager to marry. She enjoyed the admiring glances of the men in the market place. The exotic merchants flirted with her to entice her to buy their goods. They fascinated her. She considered the local young men who wanted to court her as weak and boring. She craved excitement far away from dusty Haran.

Her dark eyes would flash beneath her thick lashes and the white even teeth of her smile were alluring. Her hair was coal black with curls that bounced as she walked. Zehra dreamed of running away with one of those exotic merchants who came through Haran leading a rich caravan. She dreamed that one of them would carry her away from this drab town to a fascinating land where she would be rich as a queen.

She caught the eye of the eligible men of Haran including Lot. Lot was stocky with reddish brown hair. Like Abram, he was rugged looking and his eyes squinted as if he were seeing something in the distance. She curled up her lip and turned away whenever he attempted to speak to her.

Abram and Lot became like brothers when Abram, Sarai, and Terah came to Haran. Lot's father was Terah's younger brother Haran. Despite a difference in their ages, Lot being Abram's nephew and somewhat younger, they walked companionably together over the hills, making plans, looking over the riches of their large herds, produce, and many servants.

Suddenly God spoke to Abram in Haran. "Now go from your country and your kindred and your father's house to a land that I will show you. I will make of you a great nation."

Abram stopped in his tracks and looked around to see who was speaking. No one was there.

"Who are you, Lord? Why are you speaking to me?"

There was no answer. Abram sat down on a building stone. He went over and over the words he heard. The more he thought about it the more excited he became. He wanted to run and tell Terah, but something stopped him. Terah would insist that he go immediately.

Instead Abram told Lot of his message from God. Abram spoke so enthusiastically that Lot wanted to begin planning for the trip into this land immediately.

"No, not yet, Lot. I must stay with my father, Terah, who is old and near death. We will wait until he has gone to sleep with the fathers. Then we can leave Haran and begin the journey to our new land."

"Are you sure about this, Abram? Who is this god and what were his words? What did this god say to you?"

"It was a command! God spoke as a command! And I was to make a great nation somehow. Yes, I am sure! Why would God speak to me and make this promise if I were not the chosen one to take this land as my own?"

"Do you know anything about this new land? Why would this god choose it above all others? Why leave Haran or Ur? Why are they not good enough? What does this new land have that we do not have right here?"

"I do not have answers to your questions, Lot. I only have the command of my father's God of All. I have never heard such a command before, not even from a governor or a prince. It is a mystery to me, too. Perhaps that is why I feel I must follow it. It is a mystery!"

"I do not understand about mysteries. They are just ancient stories, but give no instructions. How do we follow a mystery?"

"The instructions are to 'go to a land I will show you.' And so I will obey and more instructions will surely be coming. We are first to go into the land of Canaan. That is all I know."

It was clear that Lot was worried and a little puzzled.

"There must be caravan routes we can follow so we do not get lost. I wonder if the people are friendly or hostile. I have heard that there are the Hittites not too far away. They are warriors."

Abram sat down on a building stone and pulled at his beard.

"I do not know what dialect they speak. I am sure we will be given the way to understand them. It is the land promised to me and the way is open. The promise said go, not wait. That could mean that the way might close at some time in the future. I just do not know!"

Lot sat quietly with Abram for a while. He did not wish to upset Abram but he had questions and concerns that continued to bubble up in his mind.

"Perhaps your god will speak to you again and answer these questions. Surely we are not expected to travel a strange land blind as old donkeys. What do you think is there that we should be looking for? Is it a treasure of some kind?"

"What would nomads like us do with a treasure?" laughed Abram. "We could not carry it with us. No, I think it must be something greater. A new land and a new kingdom perhaps. The promise was a land that I would be shown and create a great nation."

"A nation! That sounds like you would be a king! Would we be royalty? Or would we be slaves in another's kingdom?"

Lot shook his head.

"I can think of no other way but to be a king or a slave."

"A mystery is just that, Lot. Not to be figured out or understood at first, but to be followed in hope that we will eventually understand and be rewarded. It is a journey! An adventure!"

The more they talked about it the more enthusiastic Abram became and Lot along with him. In their minds they were already on the journey.

Lot was eager to make the beginning plans.

"Ah, then there is much to be done to prepare for the journey to this new land. First, I will gather the servants and herders, appoint leaders, and divide the tasks."

Before Abram could comment, Lot was off at a trot to find the herders in the hills and pastures. In the evening when Lot returned, Abram drew him down to sit beside him and begin the planning together.

"I applaud your efforts and everything you do will surely bring success to us, but there are other important things to be decided first."

"What other things? I have covered all I can think of. What else could there be? Surely you will handle any other plans for the journey that come up."

"Not this one, Lot. You must look for a suitable wife in Haran. She must be a good helpmate to you in this new land. She should be healthy and strong, able to bear many sons, and carry on the duties of a family, supervising servants, children, animals, the land, and bring honor to her husband."

Lot smiled.

"I do have someone in mind. I have been fascinated watching Zehra, daughter of Bethuel, in the market place and have approached her several times lately. She is yet unmarried. For what reason I do not know. Surely she will be ready soon to settle down with a husband as a woman should."

Lot did not mention to Abram that she had laughed at him, tossed her head, called him dull and stupid, and strode away to another merchant's display of goods.

But Lot was smitten and resolved not to give up. On a few previous occasions he had gone to speak to her father. He would go to him again and this time explain their plans to go to the land promised to Abram.

Zehra's father, Bethuel, was always pleased to welcome Lot into his home.

"Bethuel, my friend, I have exciting news. The God of All, as Terah called him, made a promise to Abram that he would be given this land in Canaan and that we are to journey there soon! We are gathering together a caravan of people who wish to journey with us.

"I wish to marry Zehra and take her with me on this wonderful journey. Will you give me your blessing, Bethuel? Will you speak to her on my behalf?"

Bethuel was taken aback and invited Lot to come in and sit down.

"Yes, of course I will speak to her. But Lot, I will not force her to marry anyone she does not want to marry. She has refused any suitors who have come to the door. She taunts and insults them and they go away.

"Now only strangers that she meets in the market place come for her, and of course I cannot agree to have strangers from foreign lands to join my family. I do not know what to do!"

Zehra came trotting in the door at that moment and looked at them. Her father went silent, but Lot greeted her with a nod and her name.

"Zehra, how good to see you! I hope your day has been pleasant. May I speak with you?"

"No, you may not! I have no wish to speak with you now or ever! Please go away."

She flounced into her room and yanked the curtain across the doorway. Abruptly, she hurried back out and left the house. Lot was disappointed and her father stood there shaking his head.

Lot was about to call after her and follow her, but Bethuel put his hand on Lot's arm.

"Lot, my son, she is willful and needs to be tamed, but I doubt that anyone could. Heaven knows I have tried and failed. She defies my attempts to discipline or teach her how to conduct herself as an honorable woman. She prefers the dangers of the market place and strange visitors from faraway places. She invites them to our home for a meal and encourages them to ask for her hand.

"She knows she is safe, that I will not agree to a stranger from another land. Her younger sisters weep in despair that they will never have husbands because the eldest must marry first.

"I do not know how I could convince her to marry you and settle down. If I force her, which is within my power, she will surely be nettles in your bed for the rest of your life."

But Lot could only see her attractiveness, her allure, and dreamed of her in his bed, nettles or not. A little disappointed he left Bethuel's house, determined to approach her again and again until she agreed.

Abram shook his head whenever Lot mentioned approaching her family for her hand in marriage. Sometimes Abram would plead with his god to also guide young Lot with wisdom, that he not make this foolish mistake.

He argued with Lot that Zehra could not possibly be the right one.

"But Lot, she is not a mature woman! She is just a frivolous girl with no good sense! She will be trouble to all of us and make your life a living hell. Look how she already brings anguish and dishonor to her own family. And yes, I have heard how she spurns you time and again in the market place."

Lot sighed and studied the back of his hands.

"Yes, she has done that."

Sarai approached him another way.

"My dear Lot, the journey into the promised land will be hard and dangerous. She is accustomed to being pampered, wearing pretty robes and scarves, able to run home if things become not to her liking.

"These are the things she wants. Not the hard life of nomads. Not the dusty roads and difficult mountain passes. Not temporary camps and living in tents. Please, think more about these things and choose someone else."

Lot took Sarai's hand in his and got down on one knee.

"She can learn. You can teach her, Sarai. You are strong. She must mature and become strong some time!"

Sarai smiled at him, removed her hand and arose to walk a little way. Lot stood up and walked alongside her.

"Think, Lot. You will need all the help you can get throughout your whole life. It is not fair to you to not have a good helpful wife. You will have to do all the work, shoulder all the burdens. It is obvious that she will not do these things. I cannot teach someone who is unwilling to learn.

"Please, Lot. You are already trying to place the burden of her unsuitability onto my shoulders. She will only get worse. I have Abram and many others to think of in this journey we face. Others are happy to do whatever tasks they need to do. Even then my burdens will be great enough."

Walking slowly Lot ran is fingers through his hair and sighed.

"There must be a way. How can I leave without her? How can I choose anyone else? I would rather go alone."

"Lot, you cannot go alone! That is no way to live. There will be daughters in the villages we pass through. Perhaps you could consider one of those."

Sarai knew that anyone would be better than Zehra, even a village girl without wit or beauty.

She and Abram knew they could not make his decision for him, though they fervently wished otherwise. They watched him struggle, walk about wringing his hands, and going to the market time and again to catch a glimpse of her and coming back glum and moody.

Lot sat down on a bench and muttered to himself.

"Choose someone else, they have said. But how can I do that? I see no one else but Zehra. No one attracts me like she does. How can I just choose another woman and look forward to the rest of my life without her, always dreaming of her while trying to be fair to a wife that is not her? Unhappy with Zehra or without her! What is the difference?"

He could hear Abram's voice in his head.

"The difference is that dreams about her can be pleasant, but actually living with her will be a nightmare, not a dream."

After a time Abram did not continue to press Lot about this. They walked silently in the hills together, each with his own thoughts about the future. His only choice would be to refuse to take Zehra along and he could not bear to lose Lot.

# CHAPTER 2

❖⁕❖⁕❖⁕❖⁕❖⁕❖⁕❖⁕❖⁕❖⁕❖⁕❖⁕❖⁕❖⁕❖⁕❖⁕❖⁕❖⁕❖⁕❖⁕❖⁕❖⁕❖

# Terah

Terah, now white haired, bent over and lame, still hobbled into the center of the town every day to confer with the officials and merchants, which was his rightful place. He spent most of his time there and at the city gates day after day with the elders.

Sometimes he lodged with his friends in order to continue their boisterous discussions into the night. Sarai would always send a servant with food and wine for all of them.

He hiked over the hills less often now more slowly, leaning heavily on his walking stick. The spring in his step was gone, but he still had youth in his voice as he bargained loudly with the merchants and yelled at the youth than ran through the streets nearly knocking him over.

Abram and Lot waited at Haran for several more months. Terah was becoming more and more infirm. His white hair and beard were thinning, his hands were stiff and trembling, and his feet were crippled making it difficult to walk.

One evening he called Abram to his tent. He preferred living in a tent even though Abram and Sarai always provided a room in their house for him.

"My breath is short and my heart is weak. I am to leave you soon. Know that I am content. I will sleep here with my fathers. You must go on and follow the calling of our god."

Abram was saddened but not surprised. God had not spoken to him since the first time he heard that mystical voice, but he could still hear the command in his mind word for word.

"Go from your country and the house of your father to a land that I will show you, and I will make of you a great nation, and I will bless you, and make your name great. I will bless those who bless you, and curse those who curse you, and by you all the families of the earth shall bless themselves."

"I will stay with you until you sleep, my father. Surely our god will not mind that I tarry here a little longer. Since He has not spoken again, perhaps this is part of His plan."

Terah leaned close to Abram's face, eyes wide and searching.

"Perhaps our god has not spoken because you are not following his command! Why should he give you another command when you have not fulfilled the first one? I will soon free you to follow your calling. I will leave and you can go. You are a good son, Abram, and I am content that you have cared for me these last few years of my life. Now prepare to go to the land that you have been promised!"

Terah sank back on his bed, exhausted by the exertion. Abram gently placed a pillow under his father's head and pulled a robe over his shivering body.

"I will go on my journey as you will go on yours, my father. I will not forget our good years together and your wise words. Although I leave you here in body, I will carry your spirit in my heart always."

He glanced back at Terah one more time as he was leaving the tent. Terah gave a huge sigh, smiled, and closed his eyes.

Abram hesitated and turned.

"Father? Father?"

He went back and gently shook Terah, but he was limp. There was no response and no breath. Abram gathered him into his arms and wept.

He spent many days walking in the hills after Terah's death, with Lot faithfully at his side. They walked in silence and only occasionally spoke.

"I have this hole in my heart since my father died. I thought surely God would speak to me again right away. But there is still nothing. How can God desert me now that I am ready to go into Canaan?"

"Perhaps you should go back to Ur and wait. Did God also speak to you there? Might he not speak again if you are there?"

Abram sat down on a rock and pulled at his beard.

"He did not speak to me in Ur. If we go to Ur he might never speak again because I did not follow the command to go to this land that is promised. How can the promise be fulfilled if I do not go there?"

"Abram, your mind is much more complicated than mine. You always amaze me when you think aloud. I am always ready to go where you go, back to Ur or on to the land called Canaan."

Lot sank back into silence fearing that he had said too much, and broke off a weed stem to chew on.

Presently Abram arose from the rock and they walked together to the top of a hill. The wind blew their robes and there was a sweetness in the air. They looked to the east, toward Ur and then to the south toward a new and strange land. The land to the south seemed to call to Abram.

"We will go to Canaan!"

"To Canaan!"

Lot echoed Abram's words and was relieved that Abram was not angry with him.

"We must not speak of this conversation to Sarai. She would give up on me completely, certain that I have gone mad that I did not choose to take her back to Ur and her life there. I know that would be her choice.

"I have taken her from her home in Ur and am now about to do that again and take her from Haran. Oh, how I honor her courage and commitment to follow my dream and to go with me! Her faithfulness is my strength. I cannot do this without her."

Lot could not help but envy Abram his wonderful marriage to Sarai. He secretly hoped he would have a marriage like that someday, but the misgivings about Zehra being that loving faithful wife were always nagging at him in the back of his mind. He would brush those doubts away quickly and turn his thoughts to some task at hand.

Abram told Sarai that he was checking on the sheep and cattle, but she knew he was looking for his god, hoping this god would speak to him again.

"How many sheep and cattle are there today, Abram? I am sure it is the same number as yesterday and the day before that."

She was chiding him and he knew it.

"There are a few more lambs, my love. Perhaps I did not see them yesterday. Their mothers hide them, you know."

"Abram you walk with your head held high gazing at the stars, but I know you do not miss a lamb or even a pebble at your feet."

He put his arms around her and held her, reluctant to release the embrace.

"And you, my love, seem to know my every thought, but I hope not all of them. I hope I have been able to keep a few things to myself just to preserve my illusion of manly privacy."

Sarai burst out laughing.

"One day you will need to explain to me just what means!"

"Yes! When I understand it myself, perhaps I will."

"What do you think we will do now that your father is gone? Will we stay? Go back to Ur?"

She tried to keep the hope out of her voice. Abram was jolted. Her words exploded in his mind.

"Did she know of my conversation with Lot? No, of course not. Going back to Ur is on her mind and always has been."

After a few moments he answered her question.

"Spring is coming. We must leave and go to Canaan. It is God's promise and I am sure we are expected to continue on. God will speak when he wants us to do something else."

"Who or what do you believe this god is, Abram? And why has he not spoken to anyone but you? Are we not all in this plan? Surely you are not expected to go alone and start a nation by yourself! Was I not mentioned?"

Now Abram was really flustered at her questions. He had just assumed that Sarai would be part of the plan, but of course she must be. He quickly moved to answer her first question, but avoided the last one.

"It is not just my god, but God of all people and all creation. He is the god who spoke to Adam and Eve, Noah and the sons of Noah, God of the flood and all abundance in the land. He is the god of my grandfather, Nahor, and my father, Terah, from whom I learned these things."

"Well, he better start mentioning me in this plan. If I am not included I will go back to Ur."

"Sarai, my love, I would not be part of a plan that did not include you!"

"Does your god know that? Does your god know that it takes families to start a nation? Does your god know that families also have babies that grow up as part of this nation? And what if these babies do not wish to continue in that plan? Maybe they will choose to go their own way! Then what? Will he destroy us all? Bring another flood?"

Abram kissed her forehead and went to find Lot.

# CHAPTER 3

❖❖❖❖❖❖❖❖❖❖❖❖❖❖❖❖❖❖❖❖❖❖❖❖❖❖❖❖❖❖❖

# THE WEDDING

The time came to leave Haran and go forth to this strange new land. The dread had lived in the depths of Sarai's mind and heart these many months. She had not wanted to leave Ur, but she thought they would return when Terah passed.

Now Abram's god has spoken to him and she was again faced with leaving her settled life in Haran. She fervently and secretly hoped they would not go, but she said nothing. She would follow Abram, the love of her life, wherever he went.

Lot, Sarai's friends Nahor and his wife, Milcah, and all the servants began the preparations. Others from Haran were eager to join them. The younger men and women who had decided to leave Haran were happy to have someone with whom to travel.

Joshua and Rebecca and their three young children were eager to go. They had family in Jericho and property. They needed to reclaim their history and ancestry. Living among family would be essential in their later years.

Jacob and Miriam had four sons who were ready for adventure. Miriam did not want to leave her home, but they had difficulty in Haran's society because Miriam's brother had been accused of theft and was found dead in a warehouse. They had not been able to clear the family name. Hopefully, this was an opportunity for them to start over as best they could somewhere else.

Zehra was not only pretty, but petulant, and an increasing problem to her family. She was the subject of the gossip at the well where the women gathered and word spread to anyone who would listen. Lot saw his chance to try once again.

Her father, Bethuel, was desperate to stop this embarrassment to his family. He had begun to favor Lot and feared that Lot might have given up. But to his delight and relief Lot came again to pursue Zehra's hand. Bethuel was overjoyed to grant Lot's request at last.

"Yes! Yes, of course! I am delighted that you have not changed your mind, Lot my son. Yes! I will tell her tonight."

Zehra was shocked, angry, and even hysterical.

"Father! Why Lot? Why not some other man? Surely there is someone better!"

Bethuel paced around the room and angrily shouted back at her.

"No one wants you, Zehra, even the merchants who laugh at you behind your back. Everyone knows you are a disgrace!"

She turned and ran through the house, throwing things and screaming.

"I will run away with a merchant on the very next caravan. I will go far away! You will never see me again! How could you promise me to this nobody, this local, graceless, boring man!

"Lot will take you far from this place, as you have just said, Zehra, and thankfully we will never see you again. At last we will be able to live in dignity and at peace!"

"I will not marry him! I will not be a willing bride at the wedding! I will refuse him and wreck everything!"

"No, you will not misbehave, Zehra, because if you do I will tie you backward on the hind end of a donkey, parade you through the market place, and make you the laughing stock of the city!"

"Please, Father, do not make me do this. I will change. I will become the obedient daughter. I will…"

"No, Zehra. You have had your chances over and over. You will not change and we will not tolerate your temper and threats any longer. You will be at the wedding and conduct yourself as a bride should and marry Lot! Thank all the gods that he is still willing to take you!"

Sarai along with Abram continued a hearty disapproval of the marriage. Sarai was highly critical of Zehra and let her displeasure show at every opportunity, hoping to drive Zehra away before the wedding. But Bethuel locked Zehra in a room in the house so this could not happen.

Zehra in turn hated Sarai who would rule over her and all the women, and make her life miserable. Zehra was determined to return the ill favor every step of the way.

"If I am forced to marry Lot I will make his and Sarai's lives a living hell!"

The wedding of Lot and Zehra was the center of days of preparations, celebrations, and feasting. Men rushed about setting up the wedding canopy, the chuppah, tables and places to sit and feast. Women decorated the poles with ribbons and flowers. Musicians were engaged.

Zehra barely tolerated the servants fixing her hair with ribbons and arranging her wedding garments. She stood stock still ready to explode any minute.

In the ceremony her mother, Puah, had to prompt her every step of the way. She did so with a mixture of joy and regret. Happy to at last be free of Zehra who always treated her with distain, and regret that she was never able to guide her or have peace with her.

The younger sisters danced and sang at the wedding celebration, and taunted Zehra as she had always taunted them. Now they would be free to marry and flirted with all the eligible young men.

The guests were all smiling and congratulating Lot. The only one who was not smiling was Zehra. She kept a veil over her face to cover her tears and retreated to her father's home as often as possible, claiming illness or exhaustion. She snatched the ribbons from her hair, threw her wedding garments down onto the floor, shuddered and cried at the thought of Lot touching her as a husband.

"Everything will be horrible! I will run away or die! Please let me die!"

She did not speak to Lot after the wedding. She avoided him every moment that she could. She hid in the storage sheds behind the servants' quarters.

She tried to run to the market place but Lot chased her, caught her, dragged her back, and tied her to a wagon. He set a servant as guard over her. She tried to cajole the servant into removing the ropes, but the servant was faithful to Lot and terrified of Zehra. He kept his distance.

Lot was red faced and to her spoke in a low threatening voice.

"Zehra, you can make this as difficult and unpleasant as you choose, but you are my wife and we are going to Canaan with Abram. You will do your part in the work you are given to do. You will walk along peaceably with everyone or you will follow tied to the back of a wagon. I am not a violent man but it would be unwise to provoke me further."

She wanted to scream and spit at him, but immediately checked herself. She did not want to know what would happen. She had never seen him angry like this and it was frightening. She sulked while servants rushed about finishing the packing of supplies and the wagons were finally loaded.

She sobbed and rubbed her chaffed wrists.

"This cannot be happening! This cannot be happening! What can I do? I am trapped!"

Then Zehra took a deep breath and began to smile, thinking of all the ways she would harass Sarai and make life a living hell for Lot.

"They will be so sorry! I will make them all miserable and oh, so sorry."

# CHAPTER 4

## THE JOURNEY

Their caravan with fellow travelers, servants, wagons, supplies, and livestock left Haran in the early morning just at dawn. At first they walked in the cool air with great anticipation, small groups quietly chatting with each other.

Zehra walked along sullen and angry. She spoke to no one even though others tried to be pleasant to her. Sarai watched her like a hawk.

In their excitement they did not seem to notice that the land became drier and more desolate as they went farther south. The green pastures and fields almost ready for harvest abruptly disappeared behind them as they crossed a mountain pass.

The contrast became sharp and frightening. Half-starved wild animals were foraging closer and closer to them. Bleached bones of animals lay scattered beside the road.

The young sons of the travelers who had been exploring the hills and running in all directions, now kept close to the caravan for protection, wary and uncertain of what dangers lay ahead.

Zehra complained incessantly and begged Lot to abandon Abram and go back to Haran.

"Can you not see how futile this is? Abram is making a big mistake and you are following right along like a dumb sheep. We must turn back now before it is too late! We can still make it back to Haran with or without Abram."

"Abandon Abram? I will not leave Abram, Zehra! He is my kin and friend, and his god will lead us through this to greater life and riches. You will see."

"I do not see riches, just dirt and dust and animal stink! I will die here and my whole life will be wasted!"

"If your whole life is wasted, it will be because you waste it complaining. Why can you not just be content? Stop complaining and just do what a wife is supposed to do for her husband and make him proud!"

"Content with what? I had a happy life in Haran and then I was forced to marry you!"

"Well, why did you not run away with a caravan as you always said you wanted to do? Would they put up with your bad temper? No, they would leave you in an arroyo in the desert to scream your head off and be eaten by jackals!"

"I will leave you and I will walk back to Haran myself!"

She turned to look back toward Haran.

"Then go, if you want too! May the wild animals get you and eat you, as they surely will. Your bones will lie along the road with theirs!"

Their shouts could be heard throughout the camp night after night.

Zehra looked back toward Haran with longing many times, but knew she would not make it alive, nor would she be welcomed by family if she did. There was nothing but to go on with Lot, Abram, and the hateful Sarai.

During the day Sarai hounded Zehra, being sure she kept to her chores and tasks. She complained to Abram.

"We told Lot not to marry her. We warned him that she would be trouble!"

Abram had no answer, no words to comfort her. He just sighed and ran his hand over his large beard.

"I know. I know."

He had only his anticipation for the next message from God to urge him forward. Surely that message would come soon now that they are on the journey God commanded.

They came to a fork in the road and a sign anchored in a rock pile that pointed the way to Damascus. Lot stood looking at the two choices.

"Would we be wise to go on to Damascus? Surely there are plenty of supplies there. It may be far enough away that the drought has not affected it so much."

Abram thought for a few moments as he rested on one of the rocks beside the road.

"No, Lot. There is nothing for us in Damascus and I am told it is far out of our way. We would only have to return back here to find the caravan road again. We will continue to the south and Shechem."

Zehra's eyes lit up when she overheard Lot mention Damascus. She had heard of it from the merchants in Haran. It sounded so exciting and she anticipated getting there. She dreamed of the market places and a chance to escape this dismal life.

"When will we get to Damascus, Lot? How much further is it?"

"We are not going to Damascus, Zehra. We will be going west to Shechem as Abram has already decided."

For a moment she was struck speechless with disappointment. Then anger welled up in her and she screamed at him.

"Abram decides! Why is it always Abram? Do you not have any courage of your own? Why do you not make the decisions? I want to go there!"

Lot just stared at her.

"Why can we not go to Damascus by ourselves? Surely there are others in the caravan who would go with us! We can stay until the drought stops and enjoy a good life there."

Lot never had any clever responses to Zehra's attacks. As always he walked away to find Abram.

They passed the route to Damascus and continued west and south toward Shechem through the mountain passes along the caravan road.

Sarai followed Zehra with a switch of a branch in her hand and threatened to smack the sulky Zehra in the legs if she did not keep moving.

They climbed a narrow pass and looked down on Shechem to the south, situated below the narrow pass that cut between two mountains. Shechem appeared to be a sizeable city on this caravan route with a large market place and plenty of food brought down from the north.

The caravan waited outside the city while Abram and Lot walked among the merchant stalls and tents. They passed the caravans, looking through their wares and asking each traveler about their homeland and what the conditions were in those places.

One caravan they perused was from Egypt and the travelers with them warned Abram and Lot that there was an even worse famine between Shechem and Egypt than they had already seen.

"You will be better off to stay in or around Shechem for a few years until the rains come again. There is little or nothing to sustain you throughout the whole land of Canaan until you reach the Nile River and its tributaries in Egypt, if you make it that far."

Lot and Abram walked a short distance away to discuss what they heard.

"Shechem is possibly the last place of plenty we will encounter if we traveled on.

"Surely there are villages and people living on the land who subsist on something. This is the land promised by God."

They gathered supplies in Shechem and started south. As the travelers told them, ahead they would see only a bleak landscape, and from a high cliff there was nothing growing as far as they could see.

Lot shook his head as they trudged along.

"How could there be a famine in a land God has promised? How could you build a nation in a land that is barren and the people are starving?"

"I suppose God was tired of me waiting for Terah to pass on. Perhaps we should have come to the land He promised instead of staying in Haran, but how could I leave my father so close to his time?"

Abram gazed at the southern horizon, one hand on his head and the other shading his eyes.

"I do not know anything about your god, Abram. But surely this god knew we could not leave Terah. Do you think this famine is punishment for something? Maybe because you disobeyed?"

"He is your god too, Lot, and God of All. I cannot think that a god of good would punish a whole country I do not even know because of me.

"I do believe if I had come to this land years ago before the famine, it might have been lush and green. But then we would still have been caught in this famine just as we are now and we would have lost everything we labored for."

Lot looked around at their people and saw grim stoic looks of determination on their faces. No one was laughing or singing anymore. Zehra had not criticized him or even spoken to him for days.

"Perhaps we should return to Haran until the drought and famine are over. Surely we can do nothing without food and water. We cannot graze sheep or plant fields. We will be fortunate to survive."

"I admit it is tempting, Lot, but I must go forward and see what God had in mind calling me to come here. I disobeyed once by staying in Haran and cannot do it again. There must be something we do not understand as yet."

Zehra brightened up as she listened in on their conversations and was sure they would take the handsome traveler's advice and stay near Shechem where there was merriment and life. It would be exciting to see this Egyptian man again, whoever he was.

She began to beg Lot to stay. She dogged his steps trying to convince him, promising him she would never nag him again.

"I will be the loving wife you want me to be. I will, I promise!"

Lot wanted so much to believe her, but everything about her behavior made him seriously doubt. She had been hateful to him even before and during their wedding. How could that suddenly change?

"Perhaps you will change until you get what you want and then it would end and you would be the way you have always been. Selfish and mean."

"But Lot, this journey has changed me! I am doing the work with the other women now. Tell Sarai to stop threatening me and I can be..."

"No Zehra! I will need to see the change in you for many months, even years, before I meet your demands."

"I just told you I have changed! And how can I be sure you would keep your promises?"

"You cannot. You will have to trust me. I am your husband. I provide for you. I decide what is best."

Zehra sank into a pout.

"When have you decided anything? Abram decides everything, not you."

"I have decided, Zehra! I decided to follow Abram long ago and that has not changed. I am not like you. You change your mind at every turn. You cannot be trusted."

Lot turned away and went to help Abram.

"Do you not have doubts, Abram, that this is the right way to go?"

"I feel the responsibility for all of our people weighing heavily upon me. They trust me and I must keep up my courage and my faith in the promise. I cannot allow doubts to enter my mind or I will surely stumble."

# CHAPTER 5

≈≈≈≈≈≈≈≈≈≈≈≈≈≈≈≈≈≈≈≈≈≈≈≈≈≈≈≈≈≈≈≈≈≈≈≈≈≈≈≈≈≈≈≈

# GOD SPEAKS AGAIN

Before they left Shechem, Abram heard from God again, confirming His promise.

"To your descendants I will give this land..."

"God has spoken to me! Everyone! God has spoken and the message is the same! We will continue on!"

To celebrate they gathered a few men servants and built a stone altar there to mark the place where God had spoken once again to Abram.

All were excited at the news. The camp came alive. The families and servants were re-energized to continue the journey. After their respite for a month in Shechem hardships were far from their minds. Adventure lay ahead.

Abram was elated and his step became brisk, tapping his staff on the ground as he walked among the people, seeing to the preparations and helping. Lot rounded up the herders from the hills and herding dogs moved the livestock together.

Preparations were made to continue the journey south. They packed the extra provisions purchased in Shechem, secured their belongings, and hitched animals to the wagons.

Zehra stomped around the camp and threw things onto the ground as she packed their belongings. She shouted at everyone and pushed servants aside who were trying to help.

"I want to stay here! I can do what I want! No one can make me leave! Do you hear me? I am staying! Someone here will take me in."

She started off toward the market place.

Sarai caught up with her and pulled her down to the ground by the neck of her robe.

"I will put sand and animal dung in the packs with your clothes if you do not behave and speak peaceably to everyone. Make no more trouble!"

Zehra jerked herself up to her feet and spun around, ready to attack Sarai, but Sarai already strode away. She sat down on the roll of carpet from her tent and burst into tears.

"I hate you! I hate Lot! I hate everyone and everything! I hate this stupid god that keeps talking nonsense to Abram!"

Through the spring and into summer they followed a well-traveled trade route. There were still steep mountain passes and dry valleys. They stopped in the middle of the day for rest and gathered what little food they could find to keep their supplies from running out.

The animals grazed, but the pastures were parched and the grasses were sparse and dry. The streams of water were small or completely dried up. The sun's white glare and heat became intense from the cloudless sky and beat down on them mercilessly day after weary day. Nights were hot with barely a breeze.

Abram and Lot traveled side by side, discussing the famine and inquiring of the occasional travelers what conditions might lie further south. The news was never good.

Villagers were relieved to see them move on by. The inhabitants had barely enough food to survive, much less to share with strangers. Traditional hospitality would leave them destitute. Abram and Lot understood and did not trouble them.

The hills were steep and the paths narrow. Sometimes they had to travel single file through the rocks. When they came through the passes and looked into the valleys that they hoped would be green, their hopes were again dashed. It was as brown and barren as the last one and the one before that.

The wind constantly blew sand and dirt into their faces and their feet were cracked from the hot hard-packed road. Their robes, coverings for their faces and worn sandals were all the same color of dirt and sand. They could hardly recognize each other.

They trudged on into Bethel and then to Ai. People in those villages looked worn and hopeless. Abram and Lot were disappointed that there was nothing for them at Bethel or Ai. Their animals were now skin and bone and their stores fast running out.

Still with faith in the promise, Abram and Lot stopped to build an altar of stone to mark the place where they hoped to return some day when the pastures were again green and the trees were full of fruit.

Zehra continued her litany of complaints and even railed at Abram.

"Is this the Promised Land? Where are the cities and riches, caravans and exciting markets? What kind of god sent us to this place which is forsaken by the very gods that own it? There is nothing here! Can you not see that? Nothing!"

Abram rarely spoke to Zehra but responded.

"If all you see is nothing, you have no vision, Zehra. You probably do not know what a vision is or care. Now be quiet."

Exhausted she eventually gave up fighting with Lot day and night. Her body was making some strange changes. She had no energy for anything except trudging on. When she began to be ill at the side of the road Sarai suspected Zehra was with child.

"I am sick and dying! You are all killing me and you do not even care!"

"You are not sick or dying, Zehra. You are with child."

"No!" wailed Zehra. "No, please. Not here! Not now in this horrible place!"

# CHAPTER 6

❧❧❧❧❧❧❧❧❧❧❧❧❧❧❧❧❧❧❧❧❧❧❧❧❧❧❧❧❧❧❧❧❧❧❧❧❧❧❧

# JERICHO

They turned east and clambered down the steep hills to the Jordan River where there flowed water from the Sea of Galilee. Even though the Jordan was very low, there was enough to revive them.

Everyone including the cattle rushed toward the water and fell into it neck deep in blessed relief from the dryness. The herders were glad that the water was shallow or the sheep would fall in, get waterlogged and drown. They pulled the sheep in and out of the water's edge with the help of the herding dogs to round them up.

Abram, Lot, and a few servants went into Jericho to do some trading for food and supplies, and to hear any news. No one knew if the drought would end soon. A decision needed to be made if they should continue on or wait in Jericho. God's message was a confirmation, but never detailed directions.

Zehra begged to go into the city too, but Lot said no.

"I cannot keep track of you and transact the business, too."

Regardless of how fervently she promised to stay close and quiet, she was left behind to stay in the camp. She continued to feel more and more ill, and lay in her tent.

In the night she screamed in pain clutching her abdomen. The women servants came rushing into her tent.

"What is the trouble, mistress? Are you hurt? Are you in pain?"

"Of course I am in pain you fools! Terrible pain!"

Zehra screamed and moaned, thrashing about on her sleeping mat. One servant ran out to fetch some water, a basin and some rags.

"Try to lie still, mistress. We fear you are miscarrying. If you are, it will be over soon."

"Miscarrying? Do you mean I really am with child? No! I cannot be! Not here in this godforsaken place!"

She moaned and burst into tears. Her agony went on through the night to early morning.

Late in the afternoon a servant who was a midwife confirmed it.

"Yes, there is blood. You have been with child but no longer. Lie still so the bleeding will stop or you will die."

Another servant mopped her brow and tried to soothe Zehra. She wanted to object and push her away, but she fell into an exhausted sleep almost immediately.

Sarai knew what was happening, but remained in her tent knowing the servants would take care of Zehra. Her presence would only make things worse.

Lot and Abram had stayed in Jericho at an inn to transact business. When they returned from the city, the midwife informed Lot that Zehra had miscarried.

She lay in the tent for a few days crying and loudly cursing Lot.

"You have taken me to this godforsaken land where I cannot properly care for myself! You are to blame for losing this child!"

She blamed him for the loss of the child over and over. As always Lot had no idea what to say to her or even if he could comfort her, so he stayed away, keeping close to Abram.

Joshua, Rebecca, and their three children bid everyone farewell and left Abram's camp for the city. They hurried through the streets of Jericho eager to find their ancestral home and relatives.

They asked residents up and down streets and alleys until one wizened elderly widow nodded to them.

"I am Ulai. I have lived here for many, many years. Are you family?"

"I am Rebecca and this is Joshua. We lived in Haran, but we know our ancestors are from Jericho. Is this the house of Eber, descendants of Noah?"

"We are the house of Eber, descendants of Noah."

The widow smiled a toothless grin.

"Please come in and be welcome."

Abram and Lot spent many more weeks near Jericho to slowly replenish their supplies and allow the animals to recover from their near starvation.

Zehra recovered slowly, vowing to kill Lot if he came near her again. She stayed in the servants' tents until the servants began to complain and Lot dragged her out of them back to his tent.

"Much as I would like to leave you in their tents and not have to listen to you bellowing like an old mule, I need the servants to concentrate on their work and to be happy.

"You will chase them off to hide in Jericho until we leave. I cannot continue without them and continue we will. The inhabitants of Jericho have been very hospitable to us. Entertain no hope that I would leave you in Jericho to poison their contentment."

# CHAPTER 7

❖❖❖❖❖❖❖❖❖❖❖❖❖❖❖❖❖❖❖❖❖❖❖❖❖❖❖❖❖❖❖❖❖❖❖❖❖❖❖❖

# PHARAOH'S EGYPT

Some merchants that Abram and Lot spoke with in Jericho were on their way to Egypt where there were great stores of grain and no famine. There were stories of great riches, green pastures for grazing and plenty of land.

Abram's mood brightened at the thought of plenty again.

"Surely God did not mean us to die here without food and water. Jericho is barely able to sustain itself and would not welcome us to stay longer. Perhaps God will speak to me in Egypt."

Then the doubts came, too.

"But what if God does not speak?"

Lot and Abram discussed the possibility of continuing on to Egypt, drawn by the news of plenty that would await them. Lot was elated at the prospect of plenty.

A traveler warned that there was great danger crossing into Egypt.

"Pharaoh's soldiers scrutinize everyone carefully at the border and any beautiful woman would be brought to Pharaoh for his selection. If anyone refuses Pharaoh, he would be killed immediately."

Lot was not worried. He was ready to give Zehra away if she did not stop her constant attacks on him and everyone who came close.

Abram, however, began looking at Sarai with new eyes as if seeing her for the first time and how beautiful she still was. The hardships of the journey had not marred her smooth face. She was still queenly in her demeanor. His heart sank. But they could not turn back. Surely this could not be God's plan for Sarai. God would protect them all somehow.

These thoughts greatly troubled Abram and disturbed his sleep. Lot saw the worried look on Abram's face, but knew not to ask. In fact he was sure he already understood what was on Abram's mind. How could he let Pharaoh take Sarai away? And yet if he refused, he would likely be killed. They all might be killed.

"We will take a great risk crossing the mountains and southern deserts of which the travelers speak. I wish God would speak to me here so I would know what to do. Perhaps we should travel with the caravan that is going to Egypt. They could guide us and it would be safer than crossing the desert alone."

They returned to the caravan as it prepared to leave for Egypt. The caravan belonged to a rich merchant and he had many guards. He looked doubtfully at Abram and Lot's ragtag travelers, but after hearing of their arduous journey from Haran, he decided they were honest and allowed them to travel with him. The brigands were numerous in this desert from Gaza to Egypt and the more men he had to fight them off, the better.

Still the journey was taxing, the road dusty and hot, the mountains forbidding, and the valleys dry. The desert was even worse with sand and wind cutting into any exposed skin.

Zehra turned away from Lot, sleeping among some of the women servants.

"I will die if I become with child again in this horrible place."

Lot was beyond caring one way or the other.

"Go! Sleep in the dirt. You will be safe from me wherever you are."

But Zehra knew that in the dark in their tent, that would not be true. He would take her roughly and release his anger and frustration on her body until he was spent. And she would be with child again.

Hearing the stories of the robbers and brigands, and what they did to women they captured, Zehra was fearful and again slept with Lot, quietly coming into his tent in the night. His snoring that she hated became some kind of comfort amid all the difficulties of the journey. At least she was safe for now.

He stirred and rolled over on top of her. She did not draw away but quietly endured until he was spent. She quickly fell asleep dreaming about the adventures Egypt might hold for her. Cities, markets, merchants…

As predicted the Egyptian soldiers set upon them a few miles into Egypt.

"Stop in the name of Pharaoh!"

They galloped up to the small caravan, swung down from their mounts and began sifting through the packs and belongings. Then they spotted Sarai.

"Whose is this woman? Is she married?"

They pointed their weapons at Abram. Abram stammered and hurried to explain that she was his sister.

Sarai gasped.

"Your sister? Why did you say that?"

Sarai had not been apprised of the conversations in Jericho about Pharaoh taking women into his harem.

"Hush woman before they kill us."

They lowered their weapons and left the caravan taking Abram and Sarai with them. They were lifted onto animals and led away. Sarai was white with anger at Abram for lying about her as if she were not his wife, and he could not bring himself to look at her.

It seemed a long distance to Pharaoh's court, and Abram and Sarai were too frightened and exhausted to talk.

As they approached a magnificent palace she whispered to Abram.

"What will happen to us now?"

"God will protect us. We will be all right."

Abram kept his head bowed and struggled to keep certainty in his voice.

"We do not know anything about Egyptians! Tell them I am your wife before it is too late!"

Abram, fearing for his own life, shook his head and turned away. The travelers in Jericho said Sarai would be safe in Pharaoh's harem, but he could not bring himself to tell her that. It would be of no comfort, he was sure.

They were prodded into the palace reception hall and pushed to their knees on the cool marble floor. While they waited, they said nothing. They could not understand any of what the guards said in Egyptian and were prodded with a spear if they spoke to each other.

Presently Pharaoh and his entourage swept into the room. He was tall and austere. His robes and crown glittered with gold. He took his seat on the jeweled throne before them. He glanced at Sarai who stood proudly and refused to be intimidated. Pharaoh nodded to the guards. Immediately they took her away.

Shock and anguish assailed Abram. He wanted to throw himself at the feet of Pharaoh and beg Pharaoh not to take her from him. But Pharaoh had left his throne and disappeared as suddenly as he arrived through the colorful thin veils that were fluttering in the breeze.

"You will be compensated with sheep, oxen, asses, men and women servants, and all manner of riches in payment for her."

Abram hardly heard the words of the Pharaoh's priest. He was in shock. The guards helped him to his feet. His legs were trembling so that he was not sure he could stand. A guard shook him to his senses and pointed where he was to go.

Outside in a huge stable area a caravan of riches was already being loaded. While he was gazing at the caravan and trying to comprehend all that happened, Abram was abruptly lifted onto the back of an animal and the procession began to move slowly through the gates of Pharaoh's palace yard, and back across the desert to where he encountered the soldiers at the border.

# CHAPTER 8

&#8767;&#8767;&#8767;&#8767;&#8767;&#8767;&#8767;&#8767;&#8767;&#8767;&#8767;&#8767;&#8767;&#8767;&#8767;&#8767;&#8767;&#8767;&#8767;&#8767;&#8767;&#8767;&#8767;&#8767;&#8767;&#8767;&#8767;&#8767;&#8767;&#8767;&#8767;

# SARAI IS TAKEN

Lot, Zehra, all the travelers, and the servants had never seen so great a store of goods and possessions, wagon load after wagon load coming toward them. The caravan was filled to overflowing with everything known to royally support human existence.

Zehra as ecstatic!

"Look at all this! Wonderful! Is it all ours? At last I have something to thank Sarai for!"

She began to open and sift through the bundles, trying on jewelry and pulling out silks and slippers.

Lot heard her squeals of delight, came around the wagons, and in a rage slapped her hands away them.

"Do not strike me or you will be to blame for another lost child! You cannot hit a woman who is with child!"

Lot pulled her with him to get to Abram.

45

Abram was lifted from his perch and set upon the ground. He visibly sagged, feeling weak, empty, and bereft. Lot caught him and helped him to a place to sit.

"I believed that God would somehow not let anything happen to us! I know no way to retrieve Sarai. How could I know Pharaoh would just take Sarai from me? He just came to his throne, motioned to his guards, and disappeared. I could not even speak to him. The guard just swept Sarai away!"

Brokenly, he told Lot and their people that Sarai was likely gone forever.

Zehra smirked in triumph. She was Lot's wife and he did not lie about her. She was with child again and was now glad to be the wife of Lot.

"At last I am rid of the critical, mean tempered Sarai."

She saw that Lot was scowling at her. She immediately covered her face and turned away.

"Now I will be the queen of a caravan, as I have had always dreamed!"

Their caravan began to move lowly, following the trade route for some distance until they came upon a suitable place where there were fields and water. They chose the higher ground for their dwellings and began to set up tents.

Abram kept busy from before dawn until after dark helping Lot unload Pharaoh's treasures into tents before any travelers might come by and see them. He did not want them to be targets of theft. Everyone was working to settle quickly into the encampment.

After setting up tents they built stone walls around the encampment. Eventually they would build houses and make it a home where they could live, trade with other caravans, and prosper.

Abram worked as a man walking in a nightmare. Everywhere he looked he expected to see Sarai, but she wasn't there. He carefully unpacked her clothing. Her fragrance was still in them. He sat in his tent looking at her robes day after day and in his dreams he could see her wearing them.

"We will get her back somehow, Abram. This cannot be the end. It just cannot be! Your god will bring her back!"

Lot tried to reassure Abram, but his attempt was clumsy and fell on deaf ears.

Abram had a grim but determined look on his face. As he walked around the camp, any gossip was quickly hushed. Lot knew that Zehra was spreading tales and fueling the talk. He had nothing with which to threaten her. When he told her to stop it, she just laughed and walked away.

She was with child, glorying in the riches, popular with the people for the tales she told, and was emotionally untouchable. She took on Sarai's position over the servants, children and all that Sarai commanded. She loved being a queen.

Lot and Abram went about doing business as caravans large and small went back and forth across the border. Their tribes and flocks were growing and their wealth even more.

Zehra reveled in her life among riches, traveling to exotic market places, and excitement teeming all around her. Her flirtatious ways made shopping and bargaining easy, her pregnancy not yet showing from beneath her robes.

Merchants were eager for her attention and willing to bring their prices down to get it. She artfully eluded their suggestive remarks and their hands. It was the wonderful game she loved and she always won.

Lot was angry with her and feared for her safety at the same time.

"One of these times one of those camel drivers will grab you and you will be gone, baby and all! Is that what you want? A filthy camel driver?"

Again the people in houses and tents near and far across the encampment heard their arguing and shouting day and night. They eagerly listened to her embellished descriptions of what was happening in those nights.

In their first year in Egypt Zehra gave birth to their child, Asya. It was a terrible struggle as her small body tried to expel the infant. The women servants hoisted her onto a birthing stool while she flailed and screamed at them that she was dying. They caught the child in a cloth, cut the umbilical cord and wrapped the baby securely in swaddling clothes. The head servant went to tell Lot that the child was not a son, and he wept.

"Surely the next one will be a son."

She was accustomed to men's disappointment at the birth of daughters and went back into the tent to tend Zehra who mercifully for everyone was asleep. It was many weeks before Lot acknowledged the child or spoke to Zehra.

Two years later the second daughter, Anah, was born.

Zehra snarled at him.

"There will be no son. You killed your son in Jericho when I miscarried and I am not going to give you another one."

From then on she lived alone in her own luxurious tent across the encampment from him with her servants and daughters.

Abram had waited years for God to speak, but God had not spoken to him since Shechem. Determined to learn more, Lot and Abram traveled to the great Nile River. They hired a barge and visited other towns and cities up and down the tributaries and onto the Nile River itself.

They marveled at the huge pyramids and statues dominating the landscapes. It was amazing that there were thousands and thousands of slaves continuing to build great cities and monuments.

Abram became curious about the Egyptian spiritual teachings and began to learn something of their language and their picture writing. The Egyptian priests offered teachings of prayer, ritual, and belief in a god and many gods. Abram and Lot were fascinated to sit and listen, but not sure God of All was represented among these priests and their teachings.

Lot and Abram were most interested in Egyptian rituals of prayer and communication with their gods that might help them understand the god that had spoken to Abram. They began to attend gatherings when invited and listened to teachers.

It all sounded very strange, but Abram and Lot had no other information with which to compare. When questioned, the high priest said that the wisdom of the ages was preserved in the pyramids, the key to which is held by him, known only to him.

Lot was angry and insulted.

"That snooty pile of bopkis!"

Abram laughed quietly and put his hand on Lot's arm.

"Do not to worry. When God speaks again and reveals everything to us, we will be better prepared to understand and we will not need their key known only to them."

Sarai languished for nearly five years in the harem of the Pharaoh, who had forgotten about her from the first day. Sarai was told by the guards in the harem that Pharaoh paid Abram handsomely for her. She was furious and questions tortured her.

"Did Abram sell me? Surely not! Had he a choice?"

Sarai waited thinking Abram would eventually come for her, but when he did not, she began to speak her prayers aloud. In her prayers she let it be known that she was actually Abram's wife and that plagues would come to Egypt if they did not release her.

"Oh, God of All, bring my husband, Abram, to rescue me lest plagues come upon Pharaoh's house. For you know I am promised to Abram and with him to begin a nation. I know you will not fail us and Pharaoh will suffer greatly unless I am returned."

News came to her through the other women that Pharaoh was not doing well. Plagues had indeed come to his house. Sarai spoke more loud and fervent prayers every morning and night to the God who had spoken to Abram. A guard overhearing her prayers went to Pharaoh with the news that she was Abram's wife, not his sister.

Pharaoh was enraged! How could plagues be brought by something other than their own gods? Abram had lied and now all of Egypt was in trouble.

"She has brought these plagues upon my house! Guards! Return her to Abram immediately! Banish them and all their earthly goods from Egypt! Destroy everything they built or left behind that there be nothing to show that they were ever here!"

It was early morning when Pharaoh's soldiers stormed into Abram and Lot's encampment and deposited Sarai at Abram's feet.

"Why did you not tell us she is your wife? You have cursed the house of Pharaoh! Take your wife and all that concerns you and be gone! Now! Pharaoh has so decreed!"

Everyone stood frozen where they were. No one dared move lest it provoke an attack. But the soldiers turned and galloped away as fast as they had ridden in. Everyone cheered except Zehra.

Sarai settled into the camp with a joyous Abram.

"Why did they release you? What miracle of God happened?"

"No miracle of God! When you did not come for me, I told them the truth! I prayed aloud to God that Abram, my husband, would come for me. That God would send plagues to Pharaoh's house if I were not released. The guards heard me and went to Pharaoh. The plagues were already there and he ordered them to take me back to my husband and banish us all from Egypt."

A very angry Sarai let them know that she was again in charge of all the women including Zehra and her daughters. She sat in front of Abram's lavish tent like a queen on a throne. Zehra was summarily deposed.

Sarai began to direct the servants as they packed up all the riches, gathered the flocks and readied their huge caravan to leave Egypt quickly. She knew the news that she had brought the plagues to Pharaoh and Egypt would spread and endanger them all.

She made sure they stripped Zehra's tent first, packed up her treasures, and loaded them with all that Pharaoh had given to Abram.

"Those are mine! You have no right to take them! You were not even here when I received them. They were gifts to me from generous merchants!"

"These were never yours, Zehra. They belong to Abram and to me! We paid dearly for them. You have earned nothing and you will have nothing except what Lot decides you may have. You might want to think, on our journey back to Ai and Bethel, what you can do to earn his trust and perhaps his generosity."

Zehra watched tearfully as her tent and all her beautiful treasures were taken away and loaded onto wagons and animals. Servants picked up her daughters and took them to be transported with the other children.

Again Zehra swore her oath of years ago in Haran.

"Oh, you will all be so sorry! I will see to it that you are all sorry for this! I will make your lives a living hell!"

# CHAPTER 9

~≈≈≈≈≈≈≈≈≈≈≈≈≈≈≈≈≈≈≈≈≈≈≈≈≈≈≈≈≈≈≈≈≈≈≈≈≈≈~

# THE PLAIN OF HEBRON

Lot and Abram decided the best thing now was to return to the Plain of Hebron, near where they had built an altar years ago.

"This is the land that God promised to us. God has indeed protected and prospered us greatly!"

Abram was elated as they crossed the border of Egypt and into the barren southern desert of Canaan. As they stood on Canaan soil Abram took a deep breath.

"Don't mention this to Sarai, Lot, but thanks to Pharaoh we are rich with herds of cattle, sheep, food stores, many families and many slaves. We can afford to wait out the famine now."

Lot laughed and laid his hand on Abram's shoulder.

"I would never approach Sarai in such a way. I have enough trouble with Zehra and I would not incur Sarai's wrath too!"

"Wise choice, Lot! Sarai made the sacrifice, but does not believe I sacrificed, too. She does not know my anguish. I cannot bear to lose her ever again."

"Ah," smiled Lot. "But I must thank Sarai for pulling Zehra down from her queen's throne and setting her down on the ground where she belongs. I do not know what happened or what Sarai said to her, but Zehra has been very quiet and even cooperative. It is nice and a little frightening because I never know when the real Zehra will rise up like a cobra again. Let us hope it is not soon."

Lot scratched his beard as he savored the thought that Zehra might be cooperative for a while at least.

The fertile valleys were west of Salt Sea near Ai, Bethel, and Salem. The water was plentiful and the grazing land was green and rich. The large level places were perfect for the people to settle their homes, and there was a natural fortification of high cliffs for protection.

The land was receiving a little rain now as they settled in a mountainous area on the Plain of Hebron. Its valleys were high above the arid lands and the heat below. At last they could have a permanent home, settle down, and become the nation that was promised.

In the evening Abram and Lot stood high on a hill, breathing in the fresh mountain air. Lot shook the dust from his robe and sandals.

"How wonderful it is after breathing in the sand and dust of the caravan routes and dry burned valleys!"

Abram pointed his staff toward the valley.

"Yes it is and now the work can begin."

Hadoram, a former citizen of Haran, was selected by Abram to be their overseer and he set to work immediately.

"I have already chosen sons of the people from Haran as my aides. The young men are now laying out the camps, setting up tents, and creating gathering places.

"A craftsman among us is planning and building races for the water to flow into the camps, cisterns to catch and store it, and walls for protection. Our stores of food will last until the planting and harvest of the fields."

Abram put his hand on Hadoram's shoulder.

"We are home at last!"

It did not take Zehra long to be once again angry and resentful, toiling under the critical eye of Sarai. Her days of the luxury and leisure in Egypt were a dream faded and gone.

"I am in hell again, but I will find a way to escape and make them all pay! Somehow, some way I will do it!"

But Asya, Anah, and the young people and children seemed not to care about leaving Egypt. They were happily running through the fields, taking food and water to the workers, enjoying their friends, and the laughter and singing of a happy people.

They accompanied Abram and Lot to area villages and cities, into Ai and Bethel to the markets. They sat with teachers by the village wells and Asya was thrilled to learn many new things.

Anah was shy but Asya coaxed her along. They sampled exotic foods and listened to strange languages. They could not wait to get back and tell Sarai all that they had done. Sarai would listen patiently and ask them many questions. Zehra would sulk in her tent, resenting Sarai all the more.

"Lot, you have to stop Sarai from taking my children away from me! She is always with them, telling them things about me."

"Zehra, try saying nice things to the children. They like people who are nice to them. You are critical, always finding something wrong with them."

"Well, someone needs to guide them! Someone needs to tell them how to behave!"

"They need love, Zehra, not mean words, especially from their mother."

"You know nothing! You are a bad father. You are always off with Abram."

Zehra tried to pout, but it was not very effective. Lot walked away shaking his head.

Their abundance kept expanding. Their families and flocks grew. Even though they had been one family for so long, two separate tribes eventually formed, Lot's tribe and Abram's tribe.

After several years there was not enough space for both tribes to exist peaceably or more land for expansion. More fields for crops were needed to feed everyone. The herders began to fight over the best grazing lands.

"Much as I wish it were not true, Lot, it is time to talk about the overcrowding that is happening. We are growing too large for this valley. We must separate our families into two tribes and find new locations farther apart."

They sat down in Abram's tent and Lot gave a deep sigh.

"I have been afraid it would come to this. We have never been apart since Haran. I have followed you for so many years, Abram. How will I determine where to go and how far will be far enough?"

"You can have this valley here in the mountains or the valley of the Salt Sea. They are not too far apart and yet there will be room enough. You may choose which one you want and I will be content with the other."

Zehra encouraged Lot to choose the lower valley. She was thinking of the cities where she could again live an exciting social life and better yet, be away from Sarai's prying eyes and sharp tongue.

Lot took Asya and Anah with him to explore the lush fertile valley of the Salt Sea where there would be grazing lands and markets that the trade route would offer.

Anah and Asya were now over eight and ten years old. They had lived in Egypt and then in the upper valleys of the Plain of Hebron. Asya was excited to move to a whole new place.

"When will we move here, Father? Very soon? Right now?"

Asya was elated, jumping up and down and clapping her hands.

Anah was not so eager. She looked around at the empty valley and was ready to cry.

"We will have to leave aunt Sarai and our friends. We will not be able to go with uncle Abram to Ai and Bethel, will we? What will we do here?"

Abram gladly chose to stay in the mountains and wilderness. Sarai was a little disappointed that they would not go to the lower valley, but she was at least happy that Zehra would be gone and she would have peace. She would miss Asya and Anah very much.

She had not yet become pregnant and she did not need any more of Zehra's knowing looks and glances at the belly area of her robe.

Hadoram was again challenged to create a new camp and life for the people. This is what he loved doing. He marshalled the men to begin taking down tents and moving livestock.

Lot and Abram spent many evenings in Abram's tent talking about the changes. Lot had not been separated from Abram since Haran. He had never struck out on his own in a strange country.

"I do not know how to begin a new life except on the farm. Perhaps I can use the teachings we learned to create new lives in Sodom. I do not know what we will find there among the pagans, but I can share the teachings with some of them. Surely the god who speaks to you is their god too."

"They likely have their own gods like the Egyptians. Be careful, Lot. They might think you are insulting their gods and even attack you. Take your time and get to know who you can trust."

Lot and Zehra, their daughters, their whole tribe, livestock, and supplies made their arduous way down the mountain into the lush green valley. They settled between Sodom and Gomorrah, on land he had seen and chosen when he went to the valley earlier.

Hadoram prepared the places where they would live and received them all with his usual stern face.

"I hope this is satisfactory, father Lot. Of course there is still much to do but it is a beginning."

"You have done well, even more than I expected. We will have a fine start here."

Zehra grumbled and stomped behind Lot as he was extolling the possibilities of the place.

"But I want to live in the city! I do not want to be stuck out in the country on a farm. I want to move into the city of Sodom right now."

"Zehra, we cannot live without food and land. This rich farm land is several miles north of the city where we can continue to prosper and expand the herds. Asya and Anah are still growing up and should live in a safe place with people they know and servants who care about them."

As they settled in day by day and month by month, Lot was hearing more and more about the dangers of life in Sodom. Zehra thought the dangers sounded exciting and could not wait to get a house there.

"My daughters need to grow up to be cultured young ladies, not ragged country drudges. They need to find rich husbands and have high places in the society."

"Your daughters? They are my daughters, too! You would teach them to be just like you were in Haran and Egypt. The rich men in Haran would not have a social embarrassment like you, and neither will the rich men of Sodom, if the girls turn out to be like you."

"My daughters will turn out just fine. They will not be buried in this dirty farm with sheep and sheep herders like you!"

"Like me? We are all happy here. You are the only unhappy one, Zehra. You always have been and you always will be. It will not matter where you are."

Enraged, she picked up something to throw at him, but he pushed her to the ground.

"No, Zehra, you will not throw things at me and you will not spoil our daughters!"

Hadoram had become very efficient in conducting the business of the farm, organizing the workers and setting up a small village for the families.

As the farm grew prosperous and buildings were built, caravans were beginning to stop out of curiosity in hopes of trade. Hadoram would haggle with them for goods and supplies.

Lot was delighted with how things were progressing and would send messages to Abram from time to time. They tried to keep communication going between the tribes using boys who were happy to carry them back and forth. Eventually the messages became fewer until they finally stopped.

Zehra grew to hate the farm more each day, the encampments, the drudgery and hard work. She longed for the city life. She was determined to live in Sodom and recover the life style she had been forced to leave in Haran and then Egypt.

Lot could stay on the farm. She did not care. She would go to Sodom. She would find a house there and bring Asya and Anah with her so they could learn the ways of a sophisticated society. They might even marry royalty!

# CHAPTER 10

❖❖❖❖❖❖❖❖❖❖❖❖❖❖❖❖❖❖❖❖❖❖❖❖❖❖❖❖❖❖❖❖❖❖❖❖❖❖❖

# SODOM

Zehra wasted no time in making trips into Sodom to shop, assess the city markets, and taste the social life. In the market area she met and befriended Dinah, widow of a prominent citizen of Sodom. Dinah was happy to tell Zehra about everything in the city. In the swirl of city life there were celebrations and social gatherings that thrilled Zehra.

"Will you come to my home while the heat of the day passes? I do want to hear more about your life in Egypt. I would love to go there someday. I love exotic places.

"My dear departed husband took me with him to many other lands where his businesses needed his attention. I never knew what his business was about, but I was happy to just go along and meet the people."

Dinah frequently invited Zehra to her home and they went to the markets together where she met other women of prominence. They visited each other's homes and talked about the city life. More and more this drew Zehra away from the farm she hated, from Lot and their daughters, who were now eleven and thirteen years old.

Asya was beginning her mid-teen years and demanded to go with her mother to the city to join in the merriment. She was growing up quickly, eager to experience the city life in Sodom that her mother talked about.

She had Zehra's bouncing black curls and flirty eye lashes which she used expertly to attract the merchants who were eager to flirt back and lower their prices to entice her to buy.

"Music and dancing fill the streets every evening and people come out of their houses to dance. There are young people your age who are very different from people on the farm and there are young rich men who will want to court you. You will have your choice of prospective husbands!"

Asya was enchanted! A delighted Zehra took her often to visit friends in their fabulous homes and to introduce her to their young wealthy sons.

Lot eventually agreed to have a home located in Sodom to satisfy Zehra's longing for the exciting life of the city and stop her constant nagging.

Life in Sodom was not only exciting, but extremely dangerous. The streets were full of filth and vermin. Servants dumped garbage and excrement from their windows onto the street below. Groups of young men wandered aimlessly through streets and alleys causing trouble.

But Zehra loved the undisciplined craziness of it. Lot feared it. He feared losing control of his family and losing them to some terrible mishap. Zehra had no common sense and Asya was pretty, sassy, immature, and impressionable. She looked more like her mother every day and wanted to be just like her.

He feared he had spawned a second Zehra.

"God, what have I done?"

Anah was more like Lot, rather plain with light freckled skin and reddish brown hair like Lot's. She tended toward the plump side, sturdy, and very shy. The noise and filth of Sodom frightened and confused her.

"You must see another side of life besides the farm, Anah! You can get a rich husband and live in luxury. No one on the farm is worthy of you!"

No matter how Zehra tried to encourage her to join in the dances, the excitement, wear make-up and pretty clothes, Anah preferred to stay home on Lot's land.

She liked to walk in the fields of flowers and care for the baby animals. She liked the company of Tebah, who was sweet and fun-loving. He brought baby animals to delight her and flowers from the field for her hair.

Lot hated living in the city, but he feared for the safety of his daughters and the growing household there. He spent more time in Sodom than he wanted to, keeping track of Zehra and Asya. He hired craftsmen to remodel the house more to Zehra's liking, and to be sure it was also secure. Hadoram appointed and trained an overseer for the Sodom household which was much needed.

Hadoram was running all of Lot's estates efficiently. He regularly sent business reports to Lot, listing numbers of sheep, cattle, servants, children born, lands acquired, and other business transactions. This was a great help to Lot, but still he preferred to be at the farm himself.

While in the city, Lot went often to the city gates where the older men of the city gathered. Remembering Abram's admonition about Egyptian religions, he began with the telling of Abram's messages from God and how God guided them through the famine, into Egypt, prospered them, and brought them back to Canaan. He did not share about the experiences with Pharaoh in Egypt or that the initial riches were the purchase price for Sarai.

He became well known for his adherence to Abram's God of All and the ability, through Lot and Abram's faith, to amass wealth. They were fascinated by these stories and always asked him for more.

While Lot and his family were in Sodom the servants kept the doors heavily barred. The ladders to the roof top were taken up at night, and walls seven feet high were built around the edges of the roof for safety.

Zehra was livid at all the extra precautions.

"This is all perfectly ridiculous and unnecessary. You have made a prison out of my house. I love this city and I go everywhere in it. What could possibly happen?"

Asya enjoyed thinking up ways to slip out seemingly unnoticed, but the overseer always caught her and brought her back. It was a cat and mouse game that she liked to play, trying to prove she could outsmart the overseer.

In the market places Asya would slip away from Zehra and Dinah, and go exploring on her own. Anah, who was still frightened by the crowds of strange looking foreigners stayed very close to Zehra and Dinah.

At the edge of the market Asya became curious and stepped into a narrow side street. She was appalled by the filth and stench and turned to go back.

A young man called to her from the doorway of a brothel.

"Come into my house lovely one. I will show you many delights and beautiful jewelry. You will be my favorite woman!"

He stepped out and grabbed her arm.

"Come now, do not be shy. I will not harm you."

Asya tried to pull her arm away

"Leave me alone!"

He laughed and tightened his grip.

"I can see you will be a wild one! We will have fun!"

Asya struggled as he dragged her toward the door. He slapped her hard and she screamed. She began to frantically claw at his face and kick at him. Inside the door the smell of heavy perfume and body sweat was overwhelming.

She wretched and fell against a wall. The man lost his grip and she bolted back out the door onto the street. She wildly ran as fast as she could to get back to the market, but she was running the wrong way through filthy alley after filthy alley.

She stopped at an intersection to catch her breath uncertain which way to turn next. A young man in a military tunic approached her.

"I am Cheran, aide to King Bara. You seem lost. May I help you?"

Asya did not know whether to trust him, but she could not take another step. She could barely muster a steady voice to answer.

"I am Asya, daughter of Lot and Zehra, and I am trying to get to the market place. They will be looking for me."

"Our guard house is only two streets from here. Would you like to freshen up and I will see that you are returned to them safely?"

Asya realized that she must look a mess. She could not let Zehra see her like this, so she agreed.

"The streets are filthy. My sandals are..."

"From the red marks on your arm I see that you have been in a struggle with someone. Why are you alone? Do you not know how dangerous these alleys are? Brothel owners are always grabbing young girls off the streets and making slaves of them. You were fortunate to get away."

Asya burst into sobs. He put his arm around her and led her to the safety of the guard house. He brought her a basin of water and a towel, and took her sandals to have one of his staff clean them.

"My guard will take you to the market to find your people."

Asya looked at the huge muscled guard and shrank back.

"Do not be afraid, he is my trusted aide and will not let anyone harm you, believe me. Go with him now."

Asya was doubtful, but she really had no choice. In her best adult voice she thanked Cheran.

"My father will want to reward you."

"No need. I serve the king and that is reward enough."

Feeling a little steadier on her feet, she followed the guard down the street toward the market place, hoping that Zehra and Dinah had not missed her. When she saw them and they called out to her, the guard quietly disappeared.

"Come! We found wonderful silks. Let us go to Dinah's house and we will show you how to make beautiful garments to trade with the caravan merchants."

Thankfully Zehra seemed not to notice Asya's slightly soiled robe and sandals. Asya kept the red finger marks on her arm covered by her sleeve. A servant at Dinah's who was helping her bathe and change her tunic looked at the arm.

"I fell," whispered Asya.

She was remembering Cheran's kind and handsome face and wondered if she would see him again. He was an aide to the king, so surely they would meet at some celebration or party. Hopefully.

Over time Lot observed that the people in Sodom seemed to be searching and restless. They had no direction for their lives, no interest in settled ways of business and family. They took mistresses, or visited brothels to try to enliven their useless lives by wallowing in lust. Some took to strong drink to numb their brains to escape the boredom.

Young women flaunted their breasts and hair like those in the brothels, claiming that this was their new freedom. Abortionists became rich relieving women of unwanted pregnancies.

Young men took part in pagan sexual games. In drunken revelry and unashamed of their nakedness, they climbed onto each other's backs in public. It all totally disgusted Lot.

"Abram's god seems very far away right now. I do not know how I could interest anyone here in believing anything good. Abram was partly right. They have their own gods, but they are not gods of creation. They have made gods of debauchery and sin. They worship bodies to be used for pleasure and to be discarded when used up. Nothing else seems to matter."

Lot was sickened and discouraged, ready to return to the farm and sanity. He went back the next day for a breath of fresh air and to remember what life was really about. He was eager to clean the stink of Sodom off his body and clothes, and out of his mind. How he loved his good clean farm life.

# CHAPTER 11

≈❖≈❖≈❖≈❖≈❖≈❖≈❖≈❖≈❖≈❖≈❖≈❖≈❖≈❖≈❖≈❖≈❖≈❖≈❖≈❖≈❖≈

# INVASION

Lot and Zehra were arguing on the roof of their house in Sodom and their daughters were downstairs talking over cheese, bread, and watered wine.

"Our daughters are coming back to the farm with me!"

"No they are not! You want to make sheep herders of them and I will not allow it!"

"The filth here is so deep that everyone is tainted by it. I will not have them be part of it! You can stay here, but I am are leaving with them now!"

"No.......What is that?"

The ground under Sodom shook. Lot went to the wall and looked over to see the hordes of invaders that were coming down the valley waving torches. The shouts of foot soldiers and the roar of horses' hooves were becoming deafening.

"Asya! Anah! Come up quickly!"

"What is it, Papa?"

"Hurry!"

They clambered up the rungs onto the roof as fast as they could. Lot pulled the ladder as soon as they were up and moved the hatch cover over the opening.

"It is an invasion! Hordes of soldiers coming from the north!"

Zehra stepped onto a bench to peer over the wall, screamed and shrank back.

"What can we do? Where can we hide? Should we go to the farm?"

"Too late, and they have probably already ravished the farm. We have nowhere to turn."

"Should we run to the neighbors?"

Asya was wide eyed and breathless. Anah huddled in a corner shaking and tearful.

"They will likely be slaughtered, too. No place is safe."

Lot sat down on the bench with his head in his hands and prayed to Abram's God of All.

"Lord, this cannot be happening! Please save us in the name of Abram our brother!"

"You old fool! There is no god and Abram is far away up in the mountains. What good will he be to us," raged Zehra. "You chose to come here to this valley and now look! There will be a war and everything will be destroyed."

"You mean your luxuries and the parties will be destroyed, do you not? That is all you care about! That is all you have ever cared about!"

She lunged toward him, fists flying, but Lot seized her arms was about to throw her back in disgust when he heard the troops from Sodom marching by.

Jumping onto the bench he shouted over the wall.

"Where are the soldiers from Gomorrah, Masada, and Admah?"

"All defeated! All taken as slaves or dead!"

"The hoards from the north have been conquering and pillaging for days. It is Chedorlaomer's armies!"

Hadoram came through the door and shouted up at Lot to put the ladder down. Shocked, Lot grabbed up the hatch cover and lowered the ladder.

"Hadoram! Thank all the gods that you got away! The farm, the stock, the property, the servants, are they all gone? Did the people get away? Are they alive?"

Hadoram stopped to catch his breath after running to the house and climbing the ladder. He went to look out over the wall at the approaching troops.

"I got away by pledging everything to Chedorlaomer including your house and families there and here, if he would spare us all. He looked over the stock, the location, the land, and decided to agree. He needed a place to establish his headquarters. Both of your places are ideal and he was pleased."

Lot's eyebrows shot up.

"He could have just taken everything! Why would you need to pledge everything?"

"For some reason he asked me to pledge rather than taking everything. It was very strange, but in that moment it was only that or death. I had to speak quickly so we might live!"

Lot sank down on the bench and Hadoram with him.

"What will happen to us now?"

"Captivity I am sure. Better than torture and death."

"Maybe death would be preferable. Our men, women, and children, all to be slaves? They will be ravished, beaten, spit upon and murdered! They will not even survive!"

Hadoram put his hand on Lot's shoulder.

"Chedorlaomer promised that we would be treated well if we would help enrich him, bring more prosperity to him. His generals saw this in our glorious farm and declared we should teach his farmers and herders to oversee the households the way I do."

"And you trust his word? None of this makes any sense! Why should he treat us well when we have no power to fight or resist? We will be his slaves!"

Lot knew about slavery from what he saw in Egypt and in Sodom. Men, women, boys and girls forced into the brothels and used shamefully. He looked at his wife and daughters and could only imagine what horrors would happen to them.

"How can I believe that we could trust a conqueror's word?"

"Abram's God of All. I promised him that all prosperity comes from Abram's god and we are the believers who can teach them."

Lot ran his hands through his hair, tugged at his beard and stood up.

"It would have to be God of All who brought us through the famine. Nothing less could save us then or now."

Zehra turned from Lot and Hadoram, and looked over the wall.

"We cannot be slaves! There must be a way out of this! We are rich and influential!"

"Not with King Chedorlaomer. You had better behave yourself, Zehra. None of your rages and screaming. They already have our riches and now they have us. You are nothing."

"Nothing? I am nothing?"

"Nothing! You have always been nothing and you will always be nothing. It is time you understood that."

The battle in Sodom lasted only a few days. People who fought were slaughtered. Others were herded from their homes and onto the road to the north. Soldiers prodded at them with spears and laughed loudly at their terror.

Beautiful clothes and jewelry were yanked from the bodies of the women and soon dirty torn tunics were their only clothing. They were assaulted along the roadsides and dragged into the bushes by soldiers. Men who tried to defend them were cut down by the sword and left to lay in their blood to die.

Lot's family and their servants were loaded into crude wagons and hauled away behind the staggering population on the road. Asya and Anah were sobbing hysterically. Lot put his arms around them and held them tight.

"Keep your heads down, be quiet, and do not draw attention to yourselves."

The sun beat down on the valley mercilessly and the dust kicked up by horses, soldiers, and the trudging captives was so thick one could hardly see. The filth and stench grew by the hour, choking their breath, and Lot wondered when it would ever end, much less end well.

The defeated kings of Sodom, Gomorrah, Admah, and Zeboiim had fled up into the hills west of the valley. Some of their men were screaming as they fell into bitumen pits, but there was no one to stop and pull them out.

The king of Zoar fled safely to the mountains east of the Salt Sea, taking his troops with him. He knew there was no point in fighting the rape of Sodom without any hope of victory.

King Chedorlaomer of Elam ordered that the captives be divided among the kings of the north, Amraphel of Shinar, Tidal of Goiima, and Arioch of Ellsar. They were conquered years ago and forced to serve King Chedorlaomer. He had subdued all of the areas of the north. Only when these kings pledged to serve him were their cities spared.

The captives were wide-eyed and terrified as they followed the soldiers to the different cities. The men were bound together and led into dungeons. The women were sold as slaves and children were forcibly taken from their mothers to the farms outside the cities.

Lot's family was taken to Elam to be kept under guard in houses adjacent to the palace. Much to her consternation, Zehra's friends were sent to the other cities. She decided it was time to stand up and fight.

She turned on her most flirtatious smiles and wiles, hoping to influence someone to bring them back to Elam. Even though King Chedorlaomer was fat and ugly, and smelled like his horses or worse, that didn't stop Zehra. She focused her charms on him whenever she got the chance and he was soon panting after her.

Lot was livid. He berated her constantly. He did his best to keep Asya and Anah out of sight and away from Zehra's disgusting assignations. It was almost worse than her behavior in Sodom.

Mercifully Asya and Anah were taken to the women's quarters where they would reside with young girls of the palace and be educated in the ways of women and house servant life.

Lot wished he could get a message to Abram but at the moment there was no chance. He was watched day and night, and no one was allowed near him. With his daughters away from him and Zehra being god knows where most of the time, he was alone and depressed. Questions and guilt plagued Lot every day and haunted his dreams at night. He sank deeper into depression as the months went by.

"How had this all happened? Was I wrong for choosing the valley? Should we have stayed in the mountains closer to Abram? Certainly I should have chosen a woman other than Zehra! But I was young and foolish then."

After many months he asked to be allowed to sit with the elders of the city. The officials saw no harm in allowing him to do that one day each week. Lot had given them no trouble. They were just old men mumbling about whatever came into their aged and demented minds.

He seized upon the opportunity hoping to again share something of Abram's God of All with them. He began telling them of his uncle's travels from Ur to Haran and about life in those northern cities.

The elders had not heard of Ur and Haran, and were fascinated to hear more. Lot's mood lifted and he was eager to share the stories, but was careful not to reveal too much more until he knew who could be trusted.

Shemah was a younger man who sat among the elders, very quiet, and most interested in Lot. He, too, was a captive and had not seen his home village for a very long time. He was so quiet that the guards had long since lost interest in him and paid him no attention.

Every time Lot was at the gates Shemah sought him out and plied him with questions about the Egyptians.

"Perhaps you might help me plan an escape to one of those cities!"

Lot smiled warmly at the young man. How good it felt to dream again, even if it all looked impossible.

"Those cities are very far away, my son, and I cannot help you escape. I cannot escape myself! And if we could, we would surely die in the wilderness and deserts."

Zehra succeeded in having her friends brought to Elam. When Lot learned of it he shook his head.

"God knows at what price!"

But he was happy to see people he knew, even though he had despised them in Sodom. He hoped they would keep Zehra busy and stop her from gallivanting among the officials.

He encouraged her to check on Asya and Anah, to learn more about where they were being kept and what they were doing. He was almost afraid to know.

Asya found herself thinking of Cheran, the official to the king who had rescued her. She hoped he would remember her. After the rescue she met him again at occasional parties and celebrations. Was he still in Sodom? Was he still alive or was he a slave somewhere? She could not bear the thought that he might be dead.

She occupied herself with fantasies about him and what their life might be like together. She remembered how he smiled at her and how she tingled all over when he came close to her.

She didn't know what it all meant, but perhaps that was how husbands and wives came together. She tried to ask Zehra about it, but Zehra said she was much too young to understand. That made the mystery all the more compelling.

She constantly recounted all she remembered about him. He was a government official and leader in the king's affairs. He was not tall but not too short. More like Lot. He was dark, very wealthy, strong and silent.

Asya soon came to know that any man at the parties who pursued her would soon be the object of Cheran's wrath, and be quietly disposed of by being sent far away. She was flattered and slightly frightened. No one had tried to control her or limit her freedom.

She was also secretly pleased at the attention and was careful not to be obvious with other men, thus not seen to be at fault. She was sure Cheran could and would dispatch her just as easily. It had all been so exciting and she had shivers when she thought of him.

Anah said she thought about Tebah.

"Who is Tebah? I did not hear about him in Sodom."

"Of course you did not. He lives on our father's land and works for Hadoram… or did. I guess our land is gone how. I used to walk in the fields with him and we would talk. He was very quiet and very smart. I liked him since I was a child. Of course I still am kind of young, but I am growing up, Asya. I am not a child anymore!"

Asya lost interest in the conversation, as she usually did when Anah was talking, turned to her loom, and tended to some of her lessons in weaving. She always thought Anah was plain and boring. She barely remembered Tebah, but then he was only a worker on the land. Anah could do so much better if she would just come to Sodom with her.

But now there was no Sodom she supposed, only burned buildings and dead people in the streets. Asya shuddered to remember the tramp of marching soldiers, their shouts of victory, and the destruction around the city. Was Cheran still alive? She desperately hoped he was, and maybe he would rescue her again.

Zehra and Dinah stayed close together since Dinah and her friends were abruptly brought from Shinar to Elam. Rebekah, Ziporah, Orpah, Judith, Elisheba were thrilled to be freed and to explore the palace as far as they were allowed, and to check out the guards on duty. It was fun to flirt again and be admired.

Dinah was still beautiful, queenly, and reserved. She was tall with pale skin and shiny black hair. Zehra always pushed past her reserve as no one else dared.

"Tell me everything about Shinar! Where were you kept? Were there markets there? What was it like? Did you meet any rich men there?"

"I was about to be a slave to some family but the captain of the guard saw me and took me to a place where I would be safe."

Zehra was thrilled and fascinated.

"Is he handsome? Will you be able to see him?"

"Yes, he is. We saw each other every day. And when I was to be moved, he promised he would come to Elam to see me and perhaps we could get away together."

"How exciting! Do you think he will?"

"I do not know. He is in the military and he thought his orders might bring him here. He said sometimes they do and he could volunteer for any mission to Elam."

"But how would you be able to get away? Where could you go that you would not be found and brought back?"

Dinah let down her guard a little and sighed.

"Tell me about Haran, Zehra. Maybe we could go there."

"It is a long way away up north. Maybe you would be safe. I have friends there who could hide you. Of course it is not the large busy city we are used to, but maybe it is far enough away. If you were noticed, you could go on east to Ur where Abram is from. I really know nothing about Ur except that it is between the large rivers close to the sea."

Thinking of Abram and Ur brought back the image of scolding Sarai, and Zehra changed the subject.

"Well, it is nice to dream about it anyway. When do you think we can go back to Sodom? Ever? Do you think there is anything left?"

Asya, Anah, Zehra, and Dinah kept feeling hopeful by talking about their dreams. They were thankful for not being slaves or shipped off to strange lands, but they really had no life in captivity. Just existence day after day and now year after year.

Asya was quietly making plans to run away. The boredom was unbearable. She busied herself by timing the opening and closing of the city gates and the changing of the guards. She did this over and over until she was sure they did not change. She didn't even tell Anah. It would be nice to have Anah with her, but Anah would never agree. She might even get frightened and report her.

"I have to know if Cheran is alive. I want to see what is left of Sodom."

She thought to steal a horse, but she didn't know how to ride, except for riding the donkeys when she was a child on the farm.

"How much different can it be to ride a horse, if I can get one? I can do it!"

Her excitement rose as ideas kept spinning through her mind. It had to be in the late summer when the river was still low and it wasn't too cold. She could cross the river to the other side in case they came down the road to Sodom looking for her.

"There might be strange people on that other side. Might they be Chedorlaomer's people? If they are, they could report me. What excuse can I make for passing among them so they would not notice that I was a run away?

"Following the setting sun I might get to Bethel and Ai on the other side of the low mountains. What if I do get lost? Lost is better than here!"

The scenarios kept playing in her mind day after day, working at a loom, weaving them into the pattern as she worked, until it all became real in her mind and she could see it clearly.

"I know every step so well, it will be easy. Cheran will be there when I get free. I know it! I will find him and he will find me. Please, please, Abram's god, bring me a horse at just the right time so I can escape from here and find him."

# CHAPTER 12

❖❖❖❖❖❖❖❖❖❖❖❖❖❖❖❖❖❖❖❖❖❖❖❖❖❖❖❖❖❖❖❖❖❖❖❖❖❖❖❖

# RESCUE

After almost five years Bera, the king of Sodom and Cheran his aide, came out of hiding from far to the south.

"It is time to return. I must know what has happened to my city and my people."

They hiked back north for many days toward Sodom and were shocked as they approached the city. All that was left was a charred mess throughout the city. Markets and streets were collapsed and even the stones of some buildings were burnt and split. It was deserted except for remnants of skeletons that lay scattered among the ruins.

"There is no need to go on to Gomorrah. It will be the same. Lot spoke of his uncle Abram's camp which is north and west of here. So we will go to find Abram. He might know what has happened to our people."

Cheran was his faithful aide and stayed close to him ready to fight off any attackers, man or beast. They hiked over goat paths, went from village to village. In the wilderness they were running out of food and had only the tattered clothes on their backs. They clawed their way up the cliff sides and scrambled onto the bluffs, hoping they would eventually come upon Abram's encampment.

A small mountain spring was a welcome sight. They drank deeply and spent a part of the day resting. A few shepherds living in the hills gave them pieces of bread and figs. They had not heard of the attack on Sodom or even known of King Bera.

Cheran thought it best not to mention that Bera was the king. They did indeed look like ragged travelers who had lost their way. Cheran thanked them profusely for the food and they moved on. Even though they were exhausted they pushed forward lest small groups of enemy soldiers might still be searching the area.

Night after night they fell face down on the ground and slept. One morning at dawn Cheran felt something prodding at his back. He jumped up, knife in hand, and stopped when he saw it was merely a young, red-cheeked, freckle faced shepherd boy.

The boy turned and ran, but hesitated when Cheran called out the name of Abram. He looked back at them and then continued to run in the direction of Abram's camp. Late in the morning a few of Abram's men came back with the boy. They gave the king and his aide water and helped them onto donkeys.

At the commotion Abram came out of his tent shading his eyes in the glare of the sun.

"Welcome to my camp. Come and be refreshed. Who are you?"

"This is his majesty, King Bera of Sodom, and I am his aide, Cheran."

"We have news," the king croaked, his throat parched.

A servant hastened to put a cup of wine into his hand. He drank deeply and continued.

"The kings of the north attacked the valley cities, burned parts of the cities including Sodom, and took all the people into slavery. Cheran, my aide, said your nephew, Lot, and his family might be among the captives taken north."

"Sir, King Bera and I narrowly escaped the invasion of the kings from the north and the destruction of the western cities along the Salt Sea."

The king was recovering his voice somewhat.

"We have been in hiding for over four years. The invaders have been searching for any who might have escaped. I am not sure how long they searched, but we thought it was now safe to venture out. We did not know for sure where to go to find you, but only to travel north and a little west."

Abram was now wide awake. He called his servants to tend the king and his aide in his tents immediately.

"Bring robes, sandals, wine and food! Care for their wounds and let them rest!"

The servants rushed in, bowed low to the king, and began to help King Bera and Cheran into the cool tent, to remove their ragged sandals, wash their feet. One ran out to get the items ordered by Abram.

The king looked wearily at Cheran.

"I would never have made it without you! I would be dead on the mountainside."

Cheran smiled knowing neither of them would have made it alone.

"And I would not be here without you, my king. I would have rushed into the battle at Sodom and been killed or at least taken captive. It is my honor to be with you. We are both well served."

Abram sat down a distance away to gather his thoughts. The shock of the invasion and the fate of his nephew, Lot, was overwhelming. They had not communicated for years. The servants told Sarai all that was happening and she went immediately to Abram.

"What will you do, my love? How can I help you?"

Abram took her hand and they sat quietly together.

"What would I do without you at my side? The years in Egypt that I was without you were the worst of my life. I had never been so lost and hope never to be so again. Let us pray first."

"Speak to me now, God. What am I to do? Lot is also your faithful servant. If he and his family are alive we must help them! Guide me as you always have, even when I did not know how to listen."

After many weeks of conferring with the king and sending messengers back and forth to Ai, Abram called all three hundred and eighteen of his men together to lay out what the strategy would be. There were certainly not enough of them to attack Chedorlaomer's army and his walled palace directly.

His messengers went to Salem, Bethel, and Ai asking for help, for troops to go with him to rescue the captives from Chedorlaomer.

The men began to assemble what weapons they had, prepare other provisions, and ready the animals to carry them. King Bera and Cheran came out of Abram's tent grateful to be rested, healed, and refreshed. They were eager to know the plans.

"We will go with you."

The king joined the men and preparations. Abram was about to object, but the king held up his hand.

"We must go with you! Your family is there and also my people from Sodom and others. It is my duty as king to do what I can to bring them back and to rebuild Sodom. I only hope my people are alive and there is enough left of the city to build upon quickly. The place is devastated."

The messengers returned on the run, panting and shouting that help would be given.

"Come to Ai as soon as you can and we will be ready."

With King Bera, Cheran, and a caravan of supplies, they all set out for Ai. To their surprise they were welcomed with shouts of joy. Abram was amazed at the readiness and enthusiasm of the other troops. His leaders immediately sat down to confer with the other troop leaders, to draw maps, and create the plans.

"General Shamar, how is it that you already have plans for an attack? Did you know about Sodom and the invasion?"

"Yes, we heard just yesterday. A young girl came to Ai riding into our camp on a horse stolen from the military, from one of Chedorlaomer's soldiers! She was ragged, terrified, and ready to faint when we caught her. She fell off the horse into our arms. She said her name is Asya."

"Asya? My niece! She cannot be more than eighteen years old! How on earth did she get free?"

"Then you know her?"

"Yes, her father Lot is my nephew. Our families grew up together. We traveled from Haran through Canaan during the famine, and on into Egypt in order not to starve."

Abram left out the part about Sarai being taken by Pharaoh. The memory still stabbed at his heart.

"She is very courageous! She said she had planned the escape for more than a year. A young tribune left his horse near the city gate in the evening while he went into an inn to relieve his thirst. She saw her chance, ran to the horse, climbed on, and galloped away through the city gates just as they were closing!"

Abram gasped in shock.

"She has the recklessness and the audacity of Zehra!"

"Who is Zehra? One of your goddesses?"

"Oh no! We worship one god, the God of All. Zehra is Lot's wife and Asya's mother. Zehra is quite rebellious and much trouble to Lot. I prayed that Asya would not grow up to be like her, but obviously my prayer has not yet been answered."

General Shamar laughed loudly.

"How did Lot come to marry such a woman?"

"He was besotted with her charm and beauty. Why else? Zehra was much trouble to her family and against her strenuous objections, they were happy to marry her off to Lot since we were leaving Haran and would take their troubles away with us. Sarai and I begged Lot not to marry her and make a better choice, but he was determined. Nothing would change his mind, even her rebuffs to his attempts to talk to her."

"We must speak of this God of All soon. We have harvest gods, fertility gods, victory gods, and many others so our lives will be prosperous, and we are. They serve us well."

This sounded like Egypt's many gods and Abram's thoughts scattered. He decided to save any conversation about that for a much later time. The troops of Ai and other cities might desert them if they thought their gods would not be honored by Abram.

Asya, sleepy eyed and yawning, came out of a tent when she heard the commotion. She knew that voice!

"Uncle Abram! Uncle Abram! Thanks to all the gods that you have come!"

Abram ran to Asya and embraced her.

"Child! How did you ever escape? How did they not catch you? You could have been killed!"

"I knew I would make it. Your god showed me how and gave me a horse just as the sun was blinding the guards and before the gate closed. I jumped on it and galloped away."

"Your mother and father? Anah? Are they alive?"

"Oh yes. Our overseer, Hadoram, made some deal with King Chedorlaomer about the farm and my family was saved."

"What caused you to make such a desperate escape?"

"I was bored. There was nothing to do but wait year after year. I was growing old and hated the thought that I might die there. I wanted to know if Cheran were alive and if anything was left of my life in Sodom."

"Cheran is alive. He is the aide to the king. They helped each other escape. He is a courageous young man. Evidently a good match for you!"

The both began to laugh and hug each other.

During the next week plans were made and solidified for the attack on the northern cities. Supplies were brought in from surrounding cities by the wagon load. In the evening a still somewhat weary King Bera and eager Cheran appeared from a tent.

Asya squealed and ran into Cheran's arms, kissing his cheeks over and over.

"Wait! Who is this lioness attacking me?"

"Lot's daughter, Asya, you fool! Do you not recognize me?"

"Yes, now I think I recognize the curly hair, but it has been several years since I found you in an alley in Sodom and returned you to your mother. You have grown up!"

"Of course I have grown up, silly! What else does one do? Have you also grown up, too?"

"I have, indeed. Come and tell me all that has happened."

She drew him away from the group, breathlessly pouring out the whole story of the last five years. He could hardly believe this was the little girl born in Egypt, who he rescued in the alleys of Sodom, now grown up and beautiful. Her eyes were flashing and her hands were flying as she spoke.

He grabbed her hands, pulled them to him.

"Whoa, slow down. You cannot tell me all of what happened in five years in five minutes! And I want to hear all of it."

Asya took a deep breath, laughed and leaned happily against his arm.

"So much has happened! I can hardly believe it. Now I am here and so are you. It is an answer to my prayers. It has to be uncle Abram's god helping us."

"Someone or something surely is!"

They smiled and their eyes did not leave each other's faces for a long time.

Abram, King Bera, Cheran, General Shamar and all of the troops of Abram, Ai, Bethel, and Salem began a trek north toward Damascus. Asya wanted so much to go too, but Abram convinced her to stay in Ai.

"You would definitely be a distraction and jealousies might arise among the men, my dear. They might even fight over you and kill Cheran!"

Horrified at the thought of losing Cheran again, Asya agreed to stay in Ai and wait for their return. She was still exhausted from her ordeal and the bruises she suffered when she fell off the horse several times in her desperate escape were still painful. She remembered the horse scrambling up the embankments and waiting for her at the top. It was a well-trained military horse staying with its master no matter how many times she slid off and climbed back on.

Abram's confidence was growing as plans unfolded in his mind. Details were becoming clearer.

"Along the way we will gather more men as we go to Damascus, secure more weapons there, and attack from the north southward. Chedorlaomer will not be expecting an attack to come from the north or from the cities in the south which he either destroyed or captured.

"He has surely grown old and fat, and he will be complacent. He will believe he is completely safe, having conquered many cities and large areas all around him. He will likely disperse his soldiers to their homes, keeping only a palace guard."

They crossed over the low mountains to the west to get to the main trade route and follow it north toward Damascus. They kept their weapons hidden and told people who asked about them that they were on a peaceful mission to explore far northern lands for the king.

It was only after men joined the troops and committed themselves to an oath that they were told the real mission. None could be allowed to leave and endanger the rescue mission. None objected. The excitement of possible battle was high and contagious among the young men.

It attracted them all to fight for a great cause, defeating the cruel Chedorlaomer, and releasing his captives. Perhaps they would find their own missing citizens and cousins among the captives. They were more than eager to train as soldiers and get started.

# CHAPTER 13

〜〜〜〜〜〜〜〜〜〜〜〜〜〜〜〜〜〜〜〜〜〜〜〜〜〜〜〜〜〜〜〜〜

# DAMASCUS

The enormity of Damascus was like nothing Abram had ever seen. Its buildings and walls were huge and its gates were at least a hundred feet tall. There were palaces, temples large and small, government buildings, paved streets and street lamps. Caravans were parked everywhere and the markets were teeming.

Much of his army stayed out of sight in the hills waiting to receive provisions and the signal to start south. The ones who entered the city spread out using several entrances so as not to draw the attention of the guards at the gates.

Even King Bera entered as a mere traveler to help gather information. Cheran would have preferred the king to wait safe in the hills, but he would not.

"I would not miss any part of the destruction of Chedorlaomer, even to the smallest detail! He will be in much more danger than I!"

There were always so many strangers coming in and out of the markets in Damascus that no one paid much attention to any newcomers. But General Shamar coached King Bera and Cheran on ways to walk, act, and how speak to the locals without arousing suspicion. Cheran stayed close to his king wherever they went in Damascus, walking behind him, conducting himself more like a lowly servant than a royal aide.

Zehra came storming into the women's quarters and shouted at Anah.

"Where is Asya? You tell me right now!"

Anah was shocked at the sudden demand.

"I do not know where she is! She does not tell me where she goes. But she must be here somewhere. Why?"

"No one can find her, you stupid child! Everyone is looking for her everywhere. She cannot just disappear! You must know something!"

"Asya hates me! She tells me nothing!"

"She must be here somewhere. How far could she get on foot?"

A matron who watched over the young girls smirked.

"Check the brothels, the homes, the alleys, everywhere!"

Zehra was wide-eyed, livid, and turned on the matron.

"How dare you look for my daughter in a brothel or an inn? She is a decent girl, well brought up!"

The matron knew Zehra well by now and burst out laughing.

"You could not bring up an ass well!"

The soldier who lost his horse simply procured another one from the military stables, saying his had died in the hills of snake bite. He did not want his superiors to know he was drinking and careless, not taking his horse to the stable first.

Word about the missing horse did not get to the palace. Who would suspect that Asya could take a horse? She was just a girl.

The more they questioned Anah, the more she cried and wailed,

"I do not know! Asya hates me and I hate her! She thinks I am stupid! She never tells me anything! I am glad if she is gone! I hope she is dead!"

The search went on for weeks. The guards questioned every man, woman and child, threatening them with beatings and torture. Some even lied, saying they had seen her, to avoid the beatings.

"Runaway slaves are common. They run away all the time. So why is everyone searching for her? She is probably dead in the hills somewhere, killed by wild animals or brigands!"

But no one had actually seen Asya.

Zehra soon lost interest in Asya's whereabouts and turned her attention to Dinah who had arrived from another city.

She had begun to spurn Chedorlaomer's attentions after Dinah arrived. At a banquet he took a tight hold on her arm.

"You seem to have little time for me, my dear Zehra. Where are you spending your time? Perhaps you should come to my quarters tonight. I will be expecting you."

She smiled at him and tried to pull her arm away but he did not let go.

"Be there or something might happen to you and your family."

Recovering her poise she shot back.

"I have been searching for my daughter! It seems that your guards have been negligent and she cannot be found. No one knows what happened to her.

"Do you know where she is? You should know. It is your palace and these are your guards. Have they done something to her? Have you done something with her?"

His anger and ardor heightened. He released her arm to hit her with the back of his hand, but then he had a better idea. Revenge would be so much sweeter. When he hesitated Zehra stepped back, bowed, and hurried away to her rooms.

"Guards! Go to her room and get her! Take her to the dungeon!"

Immediately the guards left the banquet room and went down the halls at a trot, their boots making a sharp pounding noise on the marble floors. They burst into Zehra's rooms and roughly escorted her out.

"Get your hands off me! What are you doing? Where are you taking me?"

"To the dungeon, lady!"

"On whose orders?"

"On the king's orders. Now move!"

A screaming, kicking, and struggling Zehra was dragged down the stone steps into the halls below. They pushed her into a rancid cell and down steps onto the slippery cold stone floor. The huge gate slammed behind her. The guards abruptly turned and left.

"I demand to see the king! You cannot do this to me! I am Zehra, wife of Lot! We are guaranteed protection! Do you hear me?"

But no one was there to hear her. She cringed at the filth around her and picked up a small stick to fend off the vermin coming out from the dark corners.

Dinah was mortified and fearful at the sudden abduction of Zehra by the guards. She had no idea why they had taken her, although she was beginning to guess. She witnessed the angry exchange between Zehra and the king.

She went immediately to the women's quarters to find and protect a very frightened Anah and took her to her own rooms. She kept the door closed and they hid in the next room.

It took many months in Damascus to quietly procure supplies, weapons, and information about Chedorlaomer's armies without arousing suspicion. They sent couriers back and forth to the troops in the hills keeping the general apprised of their progress.

Plans were made from the information they got about Chedorlaomer's holdings, armies, and positions. They listed the towns that were captured by him and their locations. They drew crude maps of those locations on scraps of papyrus and put together information about their conditions.

General Shamar set out the questions about the populations for which he needed immediate and accurate answers.

"Who will help us defeat Chedorlaomer and who will send him a warning? We need allies among these populations to guide us and help with timing to insure our success. Are they rebellious, subdued or integrated? Are they starving and their homes destroyed?"

Now that they were fully supplied, they prepared to quietly leave in small groups to a gathering point south of Damascus. There might be spies for Chedorlaomer hiding among the crowds who could have noticed them by now and would sound an alarm.

Surprise was of the essence.

# CHAPTER 14

〰〰〰〰〰〰〰〰〰〰〰〰〰〰〰〰〰〰〰〰〰〰〰〰〰〰〰

# ABRAM'S ATTACK

Six of the seasoned soldiers went out ahead as scouts to determine the accuracy of the information they gathered. They still dressed as travelers in plain garb, left their animals a few miles outside of the cities where the army could pick them up, and walked the rest of the way.

Two by two they went to each of the three cities and stayed close together, picking their way toward the center and the market areas. The outskirts of the cities were in shambles from neglect. There were starving beggars on the streets and filth was everywhere.

They listened to the conversations of the people and watched their demeanor. Their languages were different, but there were enough words common to other dialects that it was not difficult to determine what they were saying and if they were rebellious or so down trodden that they had given up.

The people in the cities and outlying villages were wary and guarded at first. The scouts got the message across to them that Abram's army was coming to rescue the captives from the south, and they would be freed as well. Soon they warmed to the idea that they could be freed from captivity, their cities would be theirs again.

As their doubts faded away their excitement exploded. The leaders were ready to volunteer to help Abram's army, giving directions and valuable information about the terrain.

The army was divided into three sections. One third moved into the cities and villages that were rebelling against Chedorlaomer, quietly seeking their leaders. Some of the leaders were still reluctant to come forward until their people came to them with more information about the mission of the army and assured the leaders that it was their best chance to be free.

Another part of the army moved into the oppressed areas and were met by their scouts. They offered food and assistance to the people, quietly dispatching Chedorlaomer's spies as they were covertly pointed out.

They kept chipping away at Chedorlaomer's boundaries and support until it seemed that the best time to attack Elam directly had arrived.

General Shamar directed the army groups to pull together into a main core and prepare for an all-out assault on Elam and Chedorlaomer's palace.

"We will quietly sweep down on Elam and the palace in the middle of the night, moving into the streets and alleys, armed with hidden weapons. No noise. We will light torches only when we get inside. Our scouts will come in with the rebels who are willing and able to fight."

Chedorlaomer's neighboring kings who had ridden with him to destroy Sodom and the other western cities of the Salt Sea valley were easily convinced to take their guards and disappear. They had been cheated of what they felt was their share of spoils and lost half of their soldiers in Chedorlaomer's other wars. They had no resources left to be of help. They quickly traveled to the mountains to the east and hid until the attack on Elam was over and it was certain that Chedorlaomer and his vicious ways were dead.

Local men in Elam were eager to act as guides for Abram's army and led them through the dark city streets, past barricades, and through back alleys and hidden tunnels to avoid alarming the palace guard too soon. No one was in the streets at that hour. Thanks to those who knew the layout well, Abram's army began to advance without any hindrance.

As they got closer to the palace the guard dogs began barking. The palace guards who were asleep at their posts jumped up and ran to the walls. Some climbed down to the gate and a few appeared high on the parapets of the palace.

"You down there, open the gates so the guards can go out into the streets and find what is disturbing the dogs. If they awaken the king, he will have our heads."

They thought it was a small disturbance until they saw Abram's army lighting torches and pouring through the streets and palace gates. There were not nearly enough guards overcome Abram's army. The battle was over almost before it began.

Overwhelmed, the palace guards willingly surrendered and were taken captive. The soldiers of the local army who were in their homes ran out into the streets and were immediately surrounded. They dropped any weapons they carried and quickly gave up.

The rebels dashed through the gates and down the palace halls. They found Chedorlaomer's chambers, immediately killed him, and hung his body up by the feet over the wall by the main gate for all to see and know he was dead.

In the dungeon Zehra could hear the battle cries. The guard grabbed a weapon and ran up the stairs and out into the streets.

"Guard! Guard! Let me out of here! Come back you fool! Let me out!"

The servants led Dinah and Anah to the kitchens where they hid them in their quarters behind the great hearths.

At the noise Lot woke up and bleary-eyed stumbled to a window. Someone was shouting his name.

"That sounds like Abram! Praise all the gods! Abram is here!"

He lit a lamp in the window, hurried into his tunic, robe, and sandals, and went to look for his family.

Abram and General Shamar saw the lamp and ran into the palace.

"They are still alive!"

They shouted the names of the family as they ran through hallways and stair wells.

Dinah and Anah heard Lot calling for them and came out from behind the hearth in the kitchen with the servants. He embraced a very frightened Anah.

"Where is Zehra? Is she alive?"

"Oh yes, she's alive. Very much alive! But I do not know exactly where she is. I heard that Chedorlaomer locked her in the dungeon somewhere down below."

Despite being out of breath, Lot burst out laughing.

"Why did I not think of that a long time ago? Come! A dungeon is usually somewhere under the palace or guard house."

They ran through endless halls, down dark circular stair wells, and through darker hall ways. Some halls were blocked so they had to retrace their steps and go another way.

They turned a corner, met Shamar and Abram and continued on together. Servants were running everywhere, laughing and hugging each other.

Zehra had not stopped screaming which led Lot and the others to the location of the dungeon. The smell of rats, feces, and garbage was nauseating. The problem was how to get the cell door open.

He and Abram searched the filthy floors and the hooks on the walls for the key but it was not anywhere to be found.

"You stupid men! The jailer must have taken it with him!"

Lot was out of breath and his face turned red with anger.

"Zehra, one more word out of you, and I will leave you here!"

"You cannot do that!"

"Yes, I can."

He walked away, up the stairs and out of sight.

Abram's men continued to chip away at the dungeon cell doorway. When the stones finally began to crack under the blows, it was just enough to release the spikes that held it and they pulled away.

Zehra burst out nearly knocking them down. She was still seething but wisely said nothing. She barely nodded thanks to Abram. He smiled ruefully as Zehra strode away.

Abram knew that Lot would probably not thank him either, but for a different reason.

"Poor Lot! What a pretty face and bouncing curls in Haran did to him."

# CHAPTER 15

~≈≈≈≈≈≈≈≈≈≈≈≈≈≈≈≈≈≈≈≈≈≈≈≈≈≈≈≈≈≈≈≈≈≈≈≈≈≈≈≈≈≈≈≈≈≈≈≈≈~

# THE JOURNEY HOME

It was many weeks before servants from all the surrounding small kingdoms were on their way back to their cities and their families now that they were free. Fighters from those cities who had assisted Abram's army escorted them and helped those who were ill or injured to return.

The people had been scattered over the years of captivity and servitude. Residents of those cities did what they could to help everyone find family members.

The kings, Amraphel of Shinar, Tidal of Goiima, and Arioch of Ellsar, returned from the mountains, each to his own city, to salvage what they could of normal life for themselves and the population.

Abram's army loaded the riches that had been stolen from Sodom onto their own wagons.

Chedorlaomer's wagons and beasts were used to carry many of those people who were wounded or sick south to Sodom, Gomorrah, and Admah. Some men carried the children on their backs.

The freed citizens of Elam were happy to assist the captives to organize their trek south, giving them food and water, and new sandals to protect their feet on the walk.

It was a long sad procession that began to leave the city and start down the road to what was left of their homes, but at last they were free. Songs of joy could be heard here and there along the way, and the laughter of children.

General Shamar and his troops walked along with the captives south toward the Salt Sea. Along the way they took note of the damages to the cities and villages they passed. Some parts of them were burned and other parts were still intact. Some villages were completely demolished.

In each village a designated crew of soldiers helped the men construct shelters and gather food so people coming back could eat and rest. It would be a long time before they would restore the bustling villages and cities that they were before the invasion.

Abram, Cheran and King Bera plus a few soldiers traveled back to Ai to take the spoils there from Elam, and to get Asya who was waiting probably a bit impatiently.

At their approach Asya, who was watching from a small overlook, came rushing to them and into Cheran's arms.

"What happens now? Where are we going?"

Asya was hanging on tightly to Cheran's arm.

"You can release my arm, Asya. I will not escape or disappear."

"I just want to be sure! I do not want to lose you again!"

She laughed and loosened her grip just a little, but not completely.

Abram was checking the wagons while the servants tended to the animals. He had heard Asya's question.

"We are going to Salem to tithe these spoils of war to Melchizedek, King of Salem."

"Who is he? I've never heard of him."

"I have," responded Cheran. "He is a mystery, said to be without ancestors. No one knows where he comes from, how old he is, or who his family is, if any."

Hearing this, Asya realized that there was another part of Cheran she knew nothing about.

"How do you know this?"

"King Bera told me of him. He is like a high priest, mystical and powerful. Seems to embody a likeness of the God of All. He has powers no one knows about or understands."

"What do these power do? Sounds frightening!"

"No one knows, but we are told he is always good. Nothing to worry about, Asya. You will meet him and then you can tell me what you think."

Asya shivered a little, but she trusted Cheran. She felt safe and content now that she was with him.


Abram, with some of the troops and the wagons, started for Salem. They met the other kings from Gomorrah and Admah who had fled to the mountains near Salem. They had arrived in Elam to participate in the battle against Chedorlaomer and they were ready to share their portions with Abram. But Abram refused to receive any part of the other kings' spoils of war.

"I have no need of your riches. I am already greatly prospered by the God of All. Go home and rebuild your cities. Share the riches with your people."

They looked at him quizzically.

"What god is this? Does he own your land?"

"The earth is His and everything upon it," replied Abram.

Still puzzled, King Birsha and King Sinab wished Abram well and started for Gomorrah and Admah. They discussed Abram's suggestion at length. It was a very new idea that kings should take care of the people.

"Perhaps the spoils could, indeed, be used to rebuild the cities. It would surely lift the morale of the people and make the cities prosperous again. Without our cities, we are no longer kings!"

Abram, Cheran, and Asya continued on into Salem to meet Melchizedek. The closer they got the more their anticipation grew. They asked Abram many questions about him, but Abram had the same answer to them all.

"Wait and see. He cannot be described."

Abram was correct. Melchizedek was, indeed, like no one Cheran and Asya had ever seen. He was very tall. His silvery hair and beard were long and flowing. He seemed to shimmer when he approached them and his voice was like the wind in a cave, sonorous and mysterious in origin.

Abram quickly knelt before him and was lifted back to his feet by Melchizedek.

"No need to kneel to me, Abram. You are blessed of the God of All and you will father a great nation. Your tithe is the sign of your faith in God's promise."

Melchizedek was surprisingly warm as well as ethereal.

"King Bera, it is good to see you again my friend. It has been a very long time. I know there is much work before you to rebuild your city. Call upon me and I will hear you."

Asya clung close to Cheran.

"What does he mean, he will hear him?"

"He has High Powers that we know nothing about, but he is always good."

King Bera, Cheran, and Asya fondly bid Melchizedek and Abram farewell. Reluctantly they left the peace and mystery of Salem, and started east and south toward Sodom. They journeyed carefully down steep roads and paths into the valley, quietly passing the devastation of ravaged villages knowing many must have died there.

A seemingly unending stream of people were still coming from the northern captivity, bedraggled and in shock. They were walking around the ruins looking for their families, for their homes and belongings. Sadly many found little that remained of their homes, especially in the smaller villages.

King Bera, Cheran, and Asya passed through Masada, Admah, and Gomorrah hoping their presence and the return of their kings would lift the people's spirits.

They stopped for a while in each place. The people cheered Asya as she walked among them. The story of the girl who escaped on a horse and helped to liberate them grew each time it was told. She assured them it was Abram's God of All who gave her the courage, the horse, and opened the gates of the city so she could escape.

They eagerly came to Lot's property, hoping for the best. People were still returning there. Asya saw Lot immediately. She rushed to him and tearfully embraced him.

"I am so glad you are alive, Papa!"

Anah ran to Asya and threw her arms around her.

"I never thought I would be so glad to see you!"

"I know, Anah. I have not been a very good sister all these years. I am sure you wished me dead many times."

They both laughed and held each other tight.

"And mother? Where is she, Anah?"

"Where else? In Sodom of course! She went straight there without a glance in our direction. She was driving a wagon with our possessions in it...her possessions now probably."

"But how could she get them to let her have a wagon? What happened to the driver?"

"I am sure she threatened him and scared him right off the wagon seat. He probably wanted to live and jumped for his life!"

Lot scowled at Abram as they were departing from Elam, Lot going south and Abram going to Ai.

103

"Did you have to let her out of that dungeon? You could have left her there."

"Yes, we had to, Lot. We could not leave anyone behind no matter how much we wanted to."

"You could have left *her*!"

"You could have married someone else, like Sarai and I begged you to. She's all yours, Lot."

"And, here I hoped my new life had begun. At least I will have my farm back, whatever the condition, and I will rebuild it."

# CHAPTER 16

≈≈≈≈≈≈≈≈≈≈≈≈≈≈≈≈≈≈≈≈≈≈≈≈≈≈≈≈≈≈≈≈≈≈≈≈≈≈≈≈≈

# RECOVERING THE FARM

Lot and Dinah arrived in Sodom to find that their houses were still standing. All of the belongings were taken, but much was coming back by the army wagon load. Dinah was overwhelmed at it all.

"It will be a huge task to sort out everyone's belongings among the many wagons and pack animals. Someone should be in charge of it all or there will be riots, everyone grabbing whatever they can get."

But there was no one to take charge.

When Lot found Zehra at the house, she was demanding that everyone around help unload her wagon, but most passed by without even a glance in her direction. Cursing and grumbling she began carrying the goods into the house and depositing them in areas that were somewhat clear. She was determined to restore her life in Sodom if she had to do it herself.

She demanded that Lot meet the other wagons and look for more of their goods.

"Go find our belongings or they will be stolen by all the rabble. They will take everything. Go now!

"Too bad you are not still in the dungeon, Zehra!"

Immediately he turned and walked away, took some soldiers with him and returned to his farm property to inspect the progress.

Hadoram was already working there with some of the families and were gathering the livestock they could find that had scattered or lived in the wild.

Anah was about to greet Lot when she turned and saw Tebah coming toward her from the returning captives. She ran to him and stopped short when she saw the bruises on his face and a crutch under his arm.

"Tebah, I am so happy you are still alive! I see you are hurt! What happened to you?"

"Oh, I am all right. I was not in Elam, but a slave in another city. The people there were very rough and cruel. I am fortunate that this is all I received at their hands. Many others died of their injuries, disease, and starvation."

Anah reached out and touched his cheek.

"I am so sorry. Let me help you."

She put her arm around Tebah's waist and he seemed pleased to gently lean on her.

He and Anah grew up almost like siblings, and now they were even closer. They were no longer children but man and woman.

Together they eagerly followed Lot as he began walking through the buildings and around the property. They met and spoke to the returning inhabitants about what they would need to help them now and later on. They went to work immediately, Anah caring for their wounds and Tebah on his crutch doing what he could to arrange sleeping areas to make them comfortable.

Lot went from the buildings out into the fields. Chedorlaomer had kept his word about making the place his temporary headquarters. Fields were trampled by his troops, but they could be tilled again. The families' homes were also still standing, probably used as barracks.

All things considered, the place was redeemable and it would not take very long to make the repairs. He went to the barns to gather the farm tools that were pushed into the corners and left there when the soldiers departed after the invasion. Now they could begin the work immediately.

The bedraggled crowd was still passing along the road. The families continued to come back a few at a time, running into the arms of their waiting neighbors. Hadoram took time from his work to go out and find more of the farm families.

Jacob and Miriam came running to Hadoram. They were breathless and bedraggled.

"We are so glad to see you! We have not seen Tebah. Joab and Ezra are with another group and we do not know about Shem."

"Tebah is here. He is a little battered, but Anah will take care of him."

Joab came trotting up to them.

"We have found Shem. He is quite injured and is on a litter being carried by Ezra and some others."

"Where are they? I must go to him!"

"Wait, Mother. They are coming here when they can get through the crowd. You might miss him."

Miriam kept a worried watch beside the road determined to wait for them.

"And Abigail and Merab? Does anyone know about them?"

They all looked at each other questioningly. No one had seen them. Joab anxiously turned back toward the parade of captives. He had hoped to marry Abigail one day and then the attack happened.

"I will go back and find them if I have to go all the way back to Elam!"

Hadoram shook his head.

"Two young girls alone? They may not even be alive. You are wasting time that could be spent on repairing…"

But Joab was already running back through the crowd and did not hear him.

He kept asking for Abigail and Merab as he ran mile after mile, until he sat down on a rock exhausted and discouraged. He shouted their names again and again.

An elderly woman hobbled over to him and pointed across the crowds. With a resurgence of strength from pure adrenalin he wove and struggled his way in the direction she was pointing.

An old man fell in his path. Joab stopped short and picked him up.

"Can you walk old man?"

"Yes, yes. Get my stick over there. I dropped it. I am Aram."

Joab found his walking stick and brought it to him.

"Aram, have you seen two girls named Abigail and Merab?"

Aram scratched his beard and squinted in the sinking sun as he looked around.

"There are two or three beside the road far back toward Elam. One is carrying a small child."

Joab's heart sank. A child? Is this Abigail's child? Could it be that Abigail was raped? Shocked and sickened he wanted to turn away, to go back to the farm, but something told him he could not abandon her or any of them no matter what had happened.

He stumbled on, tears running down his face. He had seen how women in captivity were treated and his heart was suddenly filled with grief.

He saw an ass afar off in a field grazing contentedly. It was unusual because asses were the exclusive property of the wealthy. They didn't run wild. He walked to it slowly, whispering soothing words as he approached. The ass paid no attention and continued to graze.

Joab tore a sleeve from his robe, fashioned a crude halter, slipped it over the asses head, and climbed on its back. It was willing to take his directions and carried him swiftly along the side of the road past the crowd of people. It would be getting dark soon. He continued to shout their names until his throat was raw and his voice barely audible.

The ass stumbled in the dark and Joab tumbled to the ground. He lay there too hungry and too tired to get up and continue. The animal stood contentedly by, occasionally poking Joab with his nose and snorting. Finally it wandered away.

In the early morning Merab and Abigail started out again, joining the parade of captives returning to Gomorrah and Sodom. Merab picked up the child and fed her the crusts of bread and whatever else the people had to share with each other. A boy was leading a goat he had caught and it supplied them with a little milk.

Joab sat up, rubbed his eyes and looked around. The long line of people still passing him seemed endless. His search seemed futile. Perhaps he should have stayed at the farm and waited. His ankle was painful when he tried to stand on it. A woman handed him a crust of bread and a few figs.

"Thank you! You are most kind."

He wolfed the food down and felt a little steadier. His voice was still feeling the strain of his shouting the day before.

"I am Joab. Have you seen Abigail and Merab, two women who are among you, one carrying a child?"

The woman who gave him the bread and figs handed him a stick to use as a crutch to ease his ankle.

"There are many young women. Come. I will help you find them."

Together they started through the crowd of bedraggled people calling their names. Joab nearly tripped over a small child that was wandering, bewildered, and looking up at everyone. Two women came rushing toward them and picked up the child.

"Abigail! Merab!"

Startled, they looked up at the call of their names.

"Joab? Joab! Is it you? Where did you come from?"

Joab could only grin and put is arms around Abigail.

"I came from home to find you."

He gently took the child from Merab.

"And who is this little one?"

"This is Josie. Her mother died at her birth. We have been caring for her."

Joab tried not to let his relief show that this was not Abigail's child. But what did it matter? Now they seemed to belong together as a family as they walked toward home together and he was content.

It was still a long walk to the farm, but they were exhilarated by being together. Even his ankle was a little less painful. A new life lay ahead of them.

"Ezra will be happy to see you, Merab."

Merab looked at Joab in shock and surprise.

"Ezra? He remembers me? He is alive? Has he come back?"

"Yes. He and I carried Shem on a litter to the farm and I came back for, uh, the two of you."

Abigail smiled at Joab's sudden correction. She knew he had come back for her.

Merab had not thought about Ezra for several years, but the thought was not unpleasant to her. Someone would be happy to see her and that teased her thoughts as she smiled and walked more eagerly.

Leah, Hadoram's wife, appeared momentarily to greet some of the returning families who were kind to her. They were happy to see her and embraced her warmly. She was shy and a little flustered at the unaccustomed caring responses from others.

She was hard working, sad faced and worn, slightly built. They had one child that died soon after its birth. Leah barely survived the birth herself. Despite Hadoram's determination to have a son, mercifully she did not conceive again. She kept to herself and slept in what was left of the sheep barn in the fields to avoid Hadoram's efforts and abuses when he was drinking.

Adam, Yaakov, and Moshe were shepherds and hunters from the farm, and were in the hills when the attack came. They took a few of the livestock as they ran away. They went to places where they used to hide as kids and kept the animals with them in case they couldn't find food. Chedorlaomer's men were scouring the hills looking for anyone who might have gotten away, but the young men were too clever for them. They knew the hills well and hid in places where no one would expect to find anything but goats.

Eventually the northern armies pulled out and headed home. Five years later coming back from hunting they ventured into the hills overlooking the farm. They saw a long caravan of people in the distance streaming down from the north, and were shocked. The people were alive!

Cautiously they started down toward the farm when they came across Hadoram who was looking for some of the livestock that might have survived in the wild.

"By all the gods, you kids are alive! I looked for you and I thought you were dead when I could not find you."

"We have been hiding for years, visiting small villages on the other side of the mountains, but no one knew where the people went. So we stayed in the hills, sharing our kills with villagers for bread and figs."

"Wait here!"

Yaakov and Moshe went back to their little camp and brought all of their food and animals to Hadoram to take to the people including their herding dogs to help him.

The four hurried down toward the farm and stopped short on a small hill. From close up the place was hardly recognizable. The buildings were still standing but some parts of them were destroyed, and the fields were trampled and flattened.

"This is what is left of our farm, Hadoram?"

"Yes, but it is enough. Let us get started."

Adam and Yaakov immediately went to work for Hadoram, gathering the pieces of debris scattered around and fashioning a corral for the animals. They put up a lean-to shelter for them at one end.

The people returning to the farm were hungry and exhausted. Moshe set up a cooking area where he slaughtered, butchered, and cooked the meat. Two men dug out the well until the water flowed and piled water jars by the well. Some were cracked and broken at the top, but Moshe filled the ones that still held some water.

Servants from the farm who returned with the procession of captives helped Moshe to prepare the food and parceled it out to the people by the side of the road. The returning captives flowed by like a river of bedraggled humanity. It was exhausting and did not end for weeks.

Wagon loads of household goods began to arrive and some rolled into the farm's main area. The loads were sorted and Hadoram gave some of the goods to each household. Slowly, they managed to create a semblance of a village. Men built and repaired buildings, women, cooked and created crude dwelling places where they could all find rest at night and have some nourishment for body and soul.

The farm people and families slowly began spread out and settle into the areas where they had formerly lived. They shared the remains of their houses to shelter others who came and planned how they would replant and rebuild their lives.

A sense of community began to take shape and everyone found something to contribute. The young girls took turns looking after Josie and other children, fashioning toys for their play and games for their amusement.

It would be a long time before things returned to normal and there was plenty for all to do, but it was a good start.

# CHAPTER 17

~◇~◇~◇~◇~◇~◇~◇~◇~◇~◇~◇~◇~◇~◇~◇~◇~◇~◇~◇~◇~◇~◇~

# SODOM REBUILDS

Eventually, Asya and Cheran went on to Sodom. Asya wanted to check on her family's home and Cheran needed to attend to the King.

On the way Cheran was quiet and Asya wondered what was on his mind.

"I wanted to ask your father for your hand in marriage, but he has much that concerns him right now, so I thought I should wait. Meanwhile, I want to ask you, would you be willing..."

"Oh yes! Yes! Yes!"

Asya didn't let him finish, but threw her arms around his neck and kissed him.

"Impulsive as always I see. I hope that never changes."

"I am my mother's daughter, sort of...but not completely. I think I am nicer."

"Please! I am depending on it!"

Zehra was grabbing clothes out of bundles and throwing things across the rooms as she sorted. She stopped as Asya appeared in a doorway.

"Well, it is about time you arrived! Is your father with you?"

Anger flashed through Asya's eyes and she barely restrained herself.

"Hello mother. Nice to see you are alive, too. No, of course father is not with me. He is restoring the farm that made the money so you could live like a queen!"

Zehra dropped what she was doing and looked hard at Asya. Asya thought her mother would strike her, but she did not.

"Well, have you come to help me since no one else will? Get busy!"

"No, I did not. But since you ask so nicely, I will. Where do you want me to start?"

Asya looked around at the near hopeless mess, probably made worse by Zehra's bad temper. She went to another room and began to arrange what was left of the furniture, throwing the broken pieces out of the window into the back courtyard, and sweeping out the dirt with a hand full of bound stiffened palm fronds.

"Where have you been? Where did you go? Do you know you got me thrown into a dungeon because you escaped?"

"Yes, I escaped, Mother, but I am sure that is not the reason you wound up in the dungeon! You were busy trying to entice Chedorlaomer, that fat smelly pig, to get your way, to get Dinah and her friends to be with you. Why, I do not know. Then when you got your way and you spurned him! What did you expect? Flowers?"

"Well it worked! I saved Dinah and her friends from a life of drudgery in that other city, whatever the name is."

"Right. Well, Dinah's gentleman lover has arrived here to be with her. She could hardly have been living a life of drudgery, as you put it. She was probably happy where she could be near him. But you would not care about that. You never cared about anyone but yourself!"

A piece of pottery hit the wall near Asya and smashed followed by angry screams from Zehra.

Asya was so disgusted that she threw the last of the broken pieces out of the window and left the house to seek out some of her friends who lived in Sodom before the attack.

Zehra was more impossible every day. Asya's eyes were open wide and she regretted how she had sided with her mother against her father all those years. She could now see what a good man her father had always been and she was overwhelmed with remorse and love for him.

"How could he ever have chosen someone like my mother, Zehra, to marry?" whispered Asya under her breath as she made her way through the rubble strewn streets.

She called out the names of her friends as she neared their homes. They appeared in doorways and rushed into the street to embrace her.

"You are alive! We feared you might be dead. Your mother would tell us nothing. She said if you were dead, it served you right."

Asya laughed and told them the story of Zehra being in the king's dungeon and of her own escape on the horse. She showed them the still visible deep bruise on her arm from falling off the horse.

"I loved that horse! He waited for me every time I fell off and tolerated my clumsy attempts to climb back on. He could have run away, but he just stood there. It must have been uncle Abram's God of All that got me through the whole thing."

"Then after you escaped you brought Abram to rescue us?"

"No, not really. He was already on his way and met more troops in Ai where I arrived the day before. He was so surprised to see me. And Cheran was with him. I was more than glad to see him!"

She regaled them with stories of meeting Melchizedek and helping at the farm. All throughout the afternoon and evening they shared their stories of where they had been taken by Chedorlaomer's soldiers and how they stuck together fending off the amorous guards.

"Dinah's guard was gentle, handsome, and smart. These others were ignorant oafs. I guess we took our freedom for granted until we lost it. But now we are so grateful to be free, alive, and together again!"

They all spent the night together at a friend's house, reluctant to part even for a few hours.

On orders of King Bera, Cheran orchestrated opening make-shift food pantries for the people. Asya and her friends worked with him to set it up and help feed the nearly starving population. It seemed as if the lines of hungry would never end, but Asya was energized working side by side with Cheran. Their compassion for the people that they never felt before grew their love for each other as well.

Anah and Tebah came in from the farm to help. They carried medicinal herbs, oils, and supplies to help the injured and sought out the elderly who could not fend for themselves. As time went on, Lot had food from his fields brought into Sodom to keep the supply full for the food pantry and the inns that still housed the sick and injured.

The cities were beginning to slowly rise out of the rubble and again commerce was building up markets and businesses. First one small caravan came. There was more curiosity than trading, but then more caravans of merchants began arriving steadily and prosperity flowed.

Hadoram had steadily rebuilt the farm and the families were thriving. Lot spent more time in Sodom supervising the building of Asya and Cheran's home, ignoring Zehra as much as possible.

No one gave a thought to Zehra except for Jahdiel, the merchant from exotic lands east of the Salt Sea, who remembered Zehra from before the attack of the northern kings. He came back again hoping to see her. He heard she had survived and knew she would need his special fabrics, exotic spices, and perfumes.

When she saw him arriving at her door she laughed, remembering her wish to run away with a merchant and live in all the luxury. But then she had the luxury without risking her freedom and safety. So she had enjoyed flirting with him, keeping just out of reach.

She was happy to see him and select from his wares, but it was not so easy to keep a distance. She needed many beautiful things to replace what had been stolen from her home. Her funds were low and he was happy to trade extra special items for her favors, as he pushed her back into her bedroom and onto the lush bed.

Zehra considered it a small thing to do for the rich rewards. He promised to come back to her home on his next trip. She would plan carefully for the next encounter. She was determined to regain control of the situation with him.

The banker and friend, Tubal, was on hand to assist Zehra with whatever funds she needed. He was a quiet and shy man. He had always pursued Zehra in covert and devious ways, but Zehra was more cunning and knew how to get money from him without giving anything away. Her flirty attention seemed to be enough. She was sure that at times she even frightened him a little and would take advantage of very subtle threating innuendo to keep him at bay.

Little by little the streets of Sodom were cleared of the rubble and burned buildings were repaired. Music and dancing returned to the neighborhoods and revelers demanded that the taverns and inns remain open far into the night. More and more women ran the taverns as travel and trade grew and they prospered along with the markets.

To Lot's consternation, the old Sodom was again booming and debauchery was everywhere. Many of the elders he used to meet at the city gate did not survive the attack and others had not yet returned to the main city gate. So he sought out other ideas and ways to begin what he had started with them.

He turned to Cheran and King Bera with his idea of building a temple alongside the food pantry. He wanted to encourage people who wanted a decent way of life in the city to come and follow the teachings that he and Abram brought from Egypt, and to worship the God of All.

King Bera was thoughtful and puzzled.

"A temple and offering food? I have not heard of these things you suggest. There has never been a temple in Sodom. Perhaps I should consult with Abram on how this might be accomplished and to learn more from the high priest Melchizedek and his disciples. He said to call upon him and he would hear. They will surely be willing to help us."

Lot's eyes lit up as he visualized the priests coming and a new way of life coming into being for the people.

"It is new for me as well, King Bera. Thank you for allowing Cheran to set up the areas for food. We need to feed and care for our people if a better way of life is to be achieved. They cannot be left in the streets with no hope.

"I will seek out the few remaining elders who met at the gate of the city. If they are well and able, they hopefully will be able to return and discuss plans about the temple. Now that the gates are restored, we can begin meeting there again, which is their tradition. I am eager to talk with them and hear the ancient wisdom that they love to share."

King Bera smiled at Lot's thoughtfulness for the people. He had always believed the people were separate from royalty and would survive or their own or not. They were never his personal concern. Now he was beginning to change his mind and see a new purpose for governing with compassion.

"I will send a messenger to you with what I have learned. I wish you success, Lot."

It was a moment to savor. The king and Melchizedek were coming together to help him and perhaps at last to transform the city, or most of it, into a civilized place, a place thriving with goodness. He closed his eyes to envision what it could be and smiled.

# CHAPTER 18

❖∼❖∼❖∼❖∼❖∼❖∼❖∼❖∼❖∼❖∼❖∼❖∼❖∼❖∼❖∼❖∼❖∼❖∼❖∼❖∼

# THE SECRET WEDDING

Zehra demanded that she be in charge of Asya and Cheran's wedding plans and reception.

"After all, I am your mother! I know how to do things properly. You are just a stupid girl. What do you know about entertaining kings and the rich?"

"Do whatever you think best, Mother. I will stay out of your way. You know how to entertain kings and I do not."

Asya kept the smile from her face and her mother did not respond to the reference alluding to Chedorlaomer. Asya knew she could not dodge the evil of Zehra this time and agreed to let her take over.

"Indeed you will stay out of it! This will be the greatest celebration the city has ever seen, not that you deserve it for escaping and leaving me in the dungeon!"

"Mother, I did not know you were in the dungeon, not that I could have done anything if I did. Someone had to get away instead of cavorting with King Chedorlaomer. Abram had to know so he could save us."

"Get out! Get out! You are an ungrateful child! I have done everything for you, clothes, jewels, and parties! And you are always insulting me! Get out!"

Asya left Zehra to her devices and began to make her own plans to have the wedding she and Cheran wanted. They wanted something traditional, quiet, and intimate, with people who loved them.

Jahdiel arrived at Asya's with beautiful silks and exotic materials for her wedding clothes. Asya was about to reject his offer, but Jahdiel quickly continued.

"I wish to thank Zehra for her business and kind attentions over the years. She had been most encouraging…uh, to my business. This is the least I can do. Please allow me and please convey to her my gratitude."

After Jahdiel bowed and departed Asya and Anah burst out laughing, knowing exactly what he meant by "kind attentions."

Dinah and Anah excitedly looked through the silks, smoothing their hands over them and exclaiming at their softness and beauty. They picked out exactly the right ones in different hues for each part of the dress and veil, and got to work immediately to create beautiful wedding garments for both Asya and Anah.

Dinah handed Anah a glass of watered wine and a pastry as they sat down together to take a break from the work. She had grown very fond of Anah throughout their captivity and her continuing association with Asya.

"Anah, I know Cheran but I do not know Tebah. He must be a good man. Will you tell me about him? I want the best for you, too."

"Oh yes! He is a wonderful man and so kind. We love each other very much. Thank you for caring about all of us. It is too bad that our mother cannot see us as you do and be kind as well. She is always screaming at everyone and it is so embarrassing."

Asya came in from talking to Cheran about the arrangements for all they would need to once again escape.

"I do not know how you can be at peace around her. My stomach gets upset and she gives me a headache. Zehra will do anything to get what she wants. I am sure she would resort to murder, and that may be on her list of ways."

Asya laughed at Anah's reference to murder. She wasn't so sure it had not already happened somewhere along the way.

"I think you are more like our father, Anah, and I am more like her, but not too much I hope!"

"Oh Asya, you have changed so much! You are more courageous than I am, and you are not mean…anymore."

"I was, Anah. I regret that."

"I love and admire you just the way you are! You have turned into a magnificent woman and Cheran is so fortunate to have you."

"And I am fortunate to have him. We came together in Ai after I escaped and nearly killed myself trying to ride a horse through mountains getting there. I knew generally the direction where Ai would be, but I think the horse knew the way for sure and got me there."

"I have your courage and your horse to thank for my freedom and Tebah's. It all turned out for the good for all of us."

Dinah loved Asya and Anah, and enjoyed her conversations with them. She loved the wedding conspiracy and promised to keep everything secret among them.

"I will soon be leaving with my beloved to go back to Elam with him. He is still a soldier in whatever military is left and desires to go home and help his people. Cheran offered him a position in King Bera's military when we return."

Asya embraced Dinah.

"Oh please, you must return to us! You must! You have been more our mother than Zehra ever was."

Zehra's household was in a flurry getting ready for Asya's wedding and making plans for a huge expensive celebration. She kept busy with the social arrangements, invitations, and ordering the wine and food. She had no interest in her daughter, only the party and making it the best gala event the city had ever seen. Flying high on excitement, Zehra bragged to everyone she met.

"My new son-in-law to be, Cheran, is a high official now and the whole city will be invited! Since Cheran is the king's aide, King Bera will be in attendance and that will bring great importance to our family in everyone's eyes. And to think that the king, himself, will be here! Everything has to be perfect for the king."

Actually everything had to be perfect for Zehra. She would stand for nothing less. The newest and largest ballroom in the city was rented and readied for the huge banquet and expensive decorations were artfully placed everywhere. Over a hundred small couches were covered with silks and large pillows. Colorful fluttery thin veils were draped gracefully in entrances and over arches. Huge vases were placed on tables awaiting the thousands of fresh flowers to be brought in just before the celebration began.

She was a bullying harridan, rushing around, overseeing every detail and shouting at the workers if they put something in the wrong place or miss-stepped in any way.

Quietly Anah and Asya gathered up the new wedding garments and carefully packed them with their clothes and belongings. They kissed Dinah goodbye and went to meet Tebah and Cheran. With the king's blessing they took the king's wagon, a few guards, and stole away in the very early dawn to Abram's camp.

Lot met them there with tears in his eyes. He knew that Zehra would literally destroy everything if the daughters were married in

Sodom. He joyfully gave his blessings for Asya to marry Cheran and for Anah to marry Tebah.

The people in Abram's camp were more than happy to create a bridal canopy of sorts and celebrate with food, flowers, dancing, and toasts to the brides and grooms. They were married by a priest of Melchizedek, with Abram and Sarai looking on. The celebration went on for several days until everyone was completely exhausted.

When they recovered somewhat from the effects of the wine and revelry, the brides and grooms, plus Abram, Sarai, and Lot went to Ai to celebrate with the friends who had helped them rescue Lot and the citizens who were taken in the attack.

They were all thrilled to see Asya again, the girl who got away on a horse, who had become almost a legend, and to meet her sister and Tebah's bride, Anah. The residents recreated the wedding canopy and the couples danced again to the music. The joy, love, and laughter were wonderful, and the celebrations were everything that they all hoped for.

Cheran and Asya took a quiet time together in a tent away from the celebrations and dancing. They were alone together at last and held each other for a long time. They made love over and over until they were exhausted and just lay together in peaceful bliss.

"Asya, what about when we return to Sodom after the wedding celebration there is over and your mother knows we were not there?"

He grinned and ran his hand over her smooth body. Asya laughed and touched his cheek.

"Some servants stood in for us in a fake ceremony. The bride would be heavily veiled and the groom bearded and covered. Zehra would never know we were not there until it was over. She would rather I were not there anyway.

"The king will be there. She will have her party and that is all she wants. I wanted to celebrate our marriage with you and the people who love us. And so we have! The added blessing was to have Anah and Tebah with us too."

"I wish my king could have been here with us, but he was happy to be complicit in the deception. He will have a private reception for us when we return."

They got up, dressed, and left the tent. Asya looked around as they walked back to the celebration.

"Speaking of Anah and Tebah, where are they?"

Cheran laughed.

"Where do you think they are, silly?"

The four of them returned with Lot to the farm and to Anah and Tebah's humble house. They walked in the fields together, breathing in the quiet pastoral atmosphere of the farm. They fed chickens and held baby lambs. They spent time with Hadoram learning about his business transactions.

It was an idyllic and carefree time for Asya and Cheran before they would return to the noise and bustle of Sodom and to Cheran's duties. Hadoram had seen to it that their house was ready for them with the last finishing touches. It was far across town from Zehra's.

Anah and Tebah continued with their lives on the farm. They were sad to see Asya and Cheran go. They had such a wonderful time, the best Asya and Anah ever had together, and promised to visit often.

Cheran went to report to the king and Asya went to their home. She arranged furniture, pillows, and vases of flowers to make it attractive and comfortable. She was warmly welcomed by the servants who were eagerly waiting there for her.

Everything was beautiful and ready for Cheran's arrival the next day. Asya went from room to room, glorying in her first very own home, touching the coverings and spreads.

She went to the front room to see if Cheran just might come home early. Her reverie was interrupted as Zehra stomped in the front door and confronted Asya. Zehra's welcome was as expected, caustic and nasty. She did not even stop to admire the house.

"You ran away to Abram to be married and left me with two impostors! How dare you insult me with your deception? You even took

Anah away from me, sneaking off in the night. I suppose she married that good for nothing sheep herder, Tebah."

"Yes, mother, I am good at escaping as you well know! You pushed me aside and created wedding plans of your own, and so you received exactly what you created. What you always create! An empty celebration of yourself!"

Zehra swung her arm to hit Asya, but a tall servant stepped between them.

"Would you care for some refreshment, madam? Wine perhaps?"

Asya stifled a smile.

Zehra turned on her heel and left as abruptly as she arrived. Cheran passed her in the courtyard and she ignored him, climbed into her carriage and screamed at the driver.

# CHAPTER 19

∻∻∻∻∻∻∻∻∻∻∻∻∻∻∻∻∻∻∻∻∻∻∻∻∻∻∻∻∻∻∻∻∻∻∻∻∻∻∻∻∻∻∻∻∻∻∻

# CHILDREN OF SODOM

Asya learned well from Zehra's artistic tastes and dressed in fabulous tunics, robes, and sandals. She became an excellent artist and decorator/designer, creating new clothing fashions and other household goods for the growing markets in Sodom.

Anah was delighted to stay with Asya a few days at a time to help with stitching, folding, and packing the items to be stored in Asya's expanding warehouse. Hadoram carefully trained the clerks that he sent to her to help market the goods.

She selected and purchased exotic silks, weaves, and other materials from Jahdiel and the many other caravans as her business grew. Jahdiel panted after Asya, attempting to draw her in as he had Zehra. Zehra used the power of her body to get what she wanted, but Asya was very different. Asya was a business woman and exhibited a queenly command.

Early in their business transactions she warned Jahdiel.

"You will keep your distance or my husband Cheran, who is now the king's commander, will deal with you harshly and if you are still alive, you will never be able to enter Sodom again."

Jahdiel quickly recognized that Asya had a kind of power that was not to be trifled with, so he maintained politeness and wisely kept to business.

Their banker and friend, Tubal, had continued to prosper with a growing banking business. He was happy to assist Asya with any financial transactions and advice. He abandoned Zehra, weary of her demanding ways, and was eternally grateful that she had never responded to his approaches. But he always loved Asya as the daughter he never had, and treated her with the utmost respect.

The city was burgeoning with life and returning to its errant ways. The women demanded more and more of the modern fashions. They sent orders to Asya for the new styles and paid handsomely for them. Even the ladies in King Bera's court made private selections at the place they referred to as The House of Asya.

Anah began bringing other young women from the farm to help with the warehouse inventories. Asya needed workers she could trust and could find no one in Sodom. The farm women were happy to help and taste a little of the exciting and exotic atmosphere of Sodom. A taste was enough. The city life was overwhelming to them and they were happy, and a little relieved, to return home to their quiet farm life.

Cheran became concerned when Asya felt unwell most mornings and stayed in bed. He was afraid she was working too hard. She could not keep food down and was tired much of the time. He brought the royal physician to see her.

The physician checked Asya over and smiled at Cheran.

"You are to be a father! May you be blessed with many strong sons!"

"And daughters!" announced Asya and Cheran in unison.

"But of course…" sputtered the physician as he took his leave.

"They will give you many grandchildren."

They were both relieved that Asya was not ill and delighted at the news. Anah sent a midwife who brought herbs to ease Asya's distress and return her appetite. Asya soon recovered from her morning sickness. After a few weeks with her energy fully returned, she continued with her garment designs while her belly grew.

Anah came more often to visit her, longing for a child of her own as well. On one of her frequent visits Anah had a miscarriage.

"I had no idea I was with child! Oh no, and now I have lost it."

She burst into tears.

The midwife was called. She told her it was fortunate that it was very early in the pregnancy and no harm was done to Anah's body. Asya suggested she stay with her a few more days and recover completely.

Anah sadly returned to the farm in a few days to tell Tebah. Again she could not hold back the tears. He put his arms around her and just held her tight.

"I am so sorry, my love."

It was a few more weeks before Anah would return to Sodom. The midwife wanted to be sure she was strong and fully recovered.

"You will have another baby, my lady, but your body must be given time to prepare itself again."

Asya was eager to see Anah and came to the farm to see how she was doing.

"It was a terrible disappointment to Tebah and to me. We wanted a child so much. We want a large family! What if we cannot have another? What if I cannot carry a child?"

"Anah, you will! Our mother lost her first one in Jericho on the way to Egypt. And she still had us! You will be all right."

"Really? Did she tell you that?"

"Oh no. She was always screaming accusations at our father, saying it was all his fault that she lost their first child. I learned a lot about their travels just from her ranting."

"If she hated our father, why did she marry him?"

"Because he wanted to marry her and her family forced her to marry him because she was temperamental, flirtatious, and wild, a disgrace to her family, just as she is now. They wanted to get rid of her and our father would take her far away from them never to return."

"Well things start to make sense. She has always done her best to make him miserable. Now I know why. I cannot imagine being anything but loving to Tebah. He is so kind and he loves me as I love him."

After a long labor Asya and Cheran's son, Dishon, was born. Asya was exhausted and happy. The midwife from the farm attended to her during her labor and after the birth to be sure all went well. Again they didn't trust anyone from Sodom.

Anah stayed by her side and delighted in her new nephew. She cradled him and sang to him. Tebah came to see the infant and to tell Anah that he missed her. She promised to come home very soon. She missed him, too.

After a few months Cheran and Asya took the infant to King Bera's palace to be blessed by the priest of Melchizedek who had married them. King Bera was delighted to hold little Dishon and coo to him. Cheran was amused to watch the king being his very human vulnerable self with the baby.

Ten months later Joktan was born to Asya and Cheran. Asya was shocked that she could be pregnant so soon after Dishon was born. The midwife told her that it often happened that way.

Again Anah was with Asya during the birth and took little Dishon home to the farm with her so Asya could rest and care for the new baby.

Anah was in heaven with an infant to care for. Soon she, too, was becoming ill in the mornings. The midwife told her that she must rest and give her body time to strengthen. Then she would not lose the baby.

Reluctantly Anah and Tebah returned Dishon to his mother and father in Sodom. They attended the blessing of Joktan and then went back to the farm.

Abram and Sarai were delighted to hear the news of the new babies and made plans to visit them in Sodom. Sarai was still without a child and had all but given up. She was aging and not sure what the promise really meant. She decided that whatever God had in mind would happen somehow. So she was able to be joyful for Asya and Cheran.

She reveled in Asya's fabulous clothing business and the beautiful silks.

"You have accomplished so much, Asya! Lot and Cheran must be very proud."

"Yes, they are! But mother is just her usual jealous spiteful self."

Lot and his guards showed Abram around the city, especially the food pantries that kept the people from starving and even now assisted the elderly. He and Abram discussed the plans for the location of the temple with the elders at the city gate. Melchizedek's priests had promised to assist with holy vestments and articles for the altar.

Abram could not help but be dismayed at the bawdiness of the women in the streets and the licentiousness of the men frequenting the many brothels. Both men and women ran naked in the streets, bragging to each other about their sexual prowess and conquests.

"I fear for you, my brother! They may tear down your temple and make a brothel out of it as well. You will need soldiers as well as guards. Place it at the edge of the city rather than in the midst, where it will be safer and decent people can come and congregate."

"I have the same concerns, Abram, but I must try. Sodom may not ever change over all, but there will be a place of hope.

"Come, let us go to the farm and I will show you all that has been done there since our return from captivity. And I still have not forgiven you for rescuing Zehra from the dungeon."

"And I have not forgiven you for marrying her!"

They both laughed as they started for the farm.

"At least you now have wonderful daughters and grandsons. Something good had to come of all your strife with her."

"I have you to thank for Asya's wisdom in not following her mother into her debauchery. Until you rescued us she hated me and acted so much like Zehra. Now she has changed and sees Zehra for what she is. And she loves me at last, a wonderful blessing for me."

"She always loved you, Lot. Zehra stood in her way and dominated her. I am happy for both of you."

Anah greeted them at the entrance to the farm. She threw her arms around Abram and kissed his cheek.

"It is wonderful to see you, Uncle! I am so glad you are here! Tebah will come in from the fields soon. We have a child coming if all goes well."

Anah's voice dropped to a whisper as her fear came back that something might happen. Lot gently lifted up her chin and embraced her.

"Anah, Anah! All will be well."

Anah smiled at them and went back to her house to rest while Abram and Lot continued to tour the farm and examine the records.

Zehra abruptly arrived at Asya's house and demanded to see the children.

"They are my grandchildren and I will see them! Where are they?"

Then Zehra came face to face with an imposing Sarai.

"You! I might have known that you would come to take my grandchildren away from me. You have already stolen Asya and Anah!"

"I have done nothing of the kind, Zehra. You drove them away with your vicious temper."

"Oh really? You and Abram welcomed them with open arms when they ran away from their wedding."

"They were not running away from their wedding. They were running away from you. They were coming to us for the quiet loving wedding they wanted. They did not want your gaudy party!"

"You turned Asya away from me! You and your sanctimonious god. A nation! You cannot create a nation! You are nothing but a dried up old…"

Sarai struck Zehra hard on the cheek. Zehra reeled backward onto a richly robed and pillowed bench. The babies began to cry and Asya rushed in to see what was happening. Worried protective servants came running, too, and picked up the children to protect them and take them to their play room.

Zehra got up from the bench and headed for the door.

"I will be back and deal with you later, Asya!"

Sarai put her arm around Asya and smoothed her hair.

"I am so sorry. I have hated her since before Lot married her. I could not help it. Zehra has not changed even with all the riches that she always wanted."

"It is not your fault, Aunt Sarai. She gets worse every year. She threatens and throws things, screaming at everyone. She cannot keep servants because she terrifies them and they disappear into the hills afraid to return. Cheran has offered to send a guard to watch over us and I have declined to have them until now. But it is time."

Lot and Abram returned to Asya and Cheran's house.

"Anah wanted to come with us but she has been advised to rest. She is disappointed not to see her aunt Sarai."

"Then I will go to her. Of course! I must not leave without seeing her."

"Cheran's guard will take you there. This city is not like your safe home in the mountains. This is Sodom and there is much danger here."

Sarai spent the rest of the day in bliss with the children, cooing to Joktan and playing with Dishon. She would wait and go to the farm in the cool of the morning, happy that at least Anah was out of Zehra's treacherous reach.

The time came for Anah to deliver her child. The midwife who had attended Asya was there, but Cheran sent the king's physician as well. Anah's labor was not overlong and she delivered a healthy baby girl. Tebah was in tears as he held them both. Anah's bleeding took a few weeks to finally stop completely and she began to strengthen.

Tebah never left her side, comforting and encouraging her.

"What shall we name her?"

He consulted family members. Then he agreed with Anah that her name should be Hannah.

Little Hannah was a strong vigorous child, waving her little fists and kicking her feet. Her hair was tinged red like Anah and Lot, and her cries were boisterous. Soon she was crawling and reaching for everything. Anah was chasing her everywhere to keep her safe.

"I thought she would be a little lamb and she is more like a tiger! She is letting us know that she can take care of herself!"

Anah and Asya spent much time together, marveling at their children's accomplishments and delighting in their playful dancing and laughter.

The sisters busied themselves designing and making a new line of children's clothing. The children would be beautifully attired and clothes for children were taken to the market along with Asya's much sought after women's designs.

Little Hannah wanted her farm clothes and pushed the pretty ones away with a resounding "No!" She preferred to follow Tebah around at the farm rather than go with her mother to her aunt Asya's.

Tebah was delighted. He doted on her and took her with him everywhere that he could, teaching her about the lambs and chicks. Hannah was thrilled to hold them and gently pet them.

It was clear to Asya that she was again with child.

"I have been feeling that morning sickness again, but thankful that it is not so bad this time."

Cheran was delighted that their family was growing, but he also wanted Asya to be healthy and safe. They discussed whether they should have more children. Cheran could sense that Asya would like to get back to her business and agreed that their three were enough.

Zehra was disgusted with Asya's growing belly.

"You are like a brood mare. You have to stop sleeping with Cheran. There are plenty of women in Sodom who would be glad to lay with him!"

Under no circumstances would she stop sleeping with Cheran! She would, however, need to learn from the midwives how to prevent further pregnancies. They had herbal potions and understood how the phases of the moon affected fertility.

Asya barely tolerated Zehra's visits to the children and had learned to ignore her opinions and nasty comments. She would not trust her mother to take the children anywhere. If Zehra gave any indication of taking the children with her, the servants were instructed to carry the children away quickly to their rooms for a nap time and guard them.

A daughter was born to Asya and Cheran. They named her Atarah after an Egyptian warrior goddess that Asya had heard about from the servants. It was the perfect name for her. Atarah asserted her independence early. She wrestled with her brothers, raced with them through the house, and refused to cry if they were too rough. She hit back.

Atarah preferred the farm style clothes like her cousin Hannah, and came back from weeks at the farm scratched and scuffed from farm work.

Asya and Anah shook their heads in dismay at their very different rough and tumble daughters.

"How could this happen, Anah? We make beautiful clothes and our daughters will have nothing to do with them!"

"Well, we will not have to worry much about them being harassed or attacked by others. They can certainly take care of themselves! Perhaps we should just be grateful."

# CHAPTER 20

~≈≈≈≈≈≈≈≈≈≈≈≈≈≈≈≈≈≈≈≈≈≈≈≈≈≈≈≈≈≈≈≈≈≈≈~

# GROWING UP
# IN SODOM

Dishon and Joktan grew up quickly, guided in right ways under Cheran's watchful eye. He took them to Lot's farm often to show them the good healthy way of life, not like life in Sodom. Hadoram taught them about the animals and crops. He took them on business trips to other farms and cities.

They stayed with their beloved Aunt Anah who so enjoyed their company. Cousin Hannah looked forward to having them come to visit, especially when Atarah came with them.

She and Atarah were fast friends and in separable growing up like Dishon and Joktan. They were curious about everything, especially when the animals were mating. They were not quite sure if people did the same thing. It was hard to imagine how that would happen. They asked some of the servant girls, who would just giggle and hurry away.

Then their thoughts quickly turned to adventures such as hiking in the hills, herding sheep with the herding dogs, and riding the donkeys. They had overheard the story of how Atarah's mother, Asya, escaped captivity on a horse and that fascinated them endlessly. They knew her only as beautiful, regal, a brilliant artist and business woman. They tried to imitate her on a horse galloping through the wilderness, but the donkeys were not very cooperative. They mostly wanted to walk and stop to nibble on grasses.

Dishon grew tall, wiry, and slim with black hair like Cheran's. He was quick witted and the girls liked him. They invited him home to dinner with their families, but he always politely declined. He enjoyed his freedom and was not about to be tied down.

Joktan was a little shorter with reddish blond hair, more similar to Lot. He was shy and always at a loss for words around the girls. He and Dishon went everywhere together and enjoyed each other's company more than the silly girls eyeing them.

They studied soldiering with King Bera's military as soon as they could be accepted into that training and much admired the fighting men. They were not like the men of the city who wasted their lives in pointless riotous living. They were tough and ready to defend the king at any time. Cheran was very proud of them. He wasn't quite sure what to do about his daughter to keep her safe.

Cheran need not have worried. Atarah, a frizzy red haired firebrand, was outspoken for women of that time and ready to defend herself wherever she was. She was not allowed to join in soldiering in the military like her brothers, but she could pass information to her father from them about military matters. She took food and supplies to them at their outposts and learned all that she could about soldiering. She hid in the rocks and watched the trainings until they saw her and shooed her away. But she would come back to watch again day after day until she could emulate the hand-to-hand combat maneuvers and imagined herself winning the battles.

She secretly carried a knife and became skilled in how to use it. She learned some things about anatomy when Hannah showed her how to skin an animal for cooking. She could see just where to strike.

The men knew better than to accost her. Some were afraid of her brothers, but mostly they were afraid of her. Proposals of marriage were not forthcoming and she was happy about that.

She often went shopping in the market place with Dishon and Joktan. When the boys went to another part of the market to inspect weapons, two men approached her grinning viciously and snarled at her.

"Maybe you are really a boy! Come here! Let us take off your clothes and prove you are a girl!"

She turned away and they grabbed her arms from behind which was their mistake. The training she watched and practiced served her well. She lurched forward thrusting her arms forward breaking their hold and then tripped them and threw them to the ground. She stood over them with feet planted firmly apart, pulled out her knife and threatened to slice them up where it would hurt the most.

Dishon and Joktan came up right behind her laughing uproariously.

"Who is a girl now you two drunken piles of sheep dung?"

Atarah stepped back and they scrambled away crawling on all fours, not able to regain their footing to run. Dishon and Joktan dragged them by their hair into an alley, beat and kicked them repeatedly until they curled up against the base of a wall and cried for mercy.

"Try that again and we will let her carve up your private parts!"

Atarah continued her shopping, but her brothers stayed close by. When they started home together Dishon was still grinning.

"Atarah! We knew you could take care of yourself, but this is the first time we have seen you in action! Where did you learn these things?"

"First from Hannah when I helped her carve up animal carcasses for cooking and then from watching the training at your military camp. I can take care of myself, but I do appreciate your backup, and please do not tell mother. She will never let me out of her sight again."

Joktan chuckled and rubbed his stubbly chin.

"Do not worry! I will not tell anyone that my sister can overpower me and throw me to the ground. It would be too embarrassing. They would start calling me a girl for sure!"

"My brothers, we are a great team and I am very proud of you both. Just be careful! I have many hidden talents."

Dishon and Joktan looked wide-eyed at each other and shrugged. They did not try to imagine what she meant.

"We will! Very careful!"

Lot and the elders chose a place for a temple on the outer rim of the city. It would not be large, but spacious enough for meetings and worship. It would be quite plain on the outside so as not to draw unwanted attention. Hadoram sent stone cutters and carpenters to begin the building.

The priests of Melchizedek brought artifacts for the altar and vestments that they collected and stored in Asya's warehouse until the temple was completed.

As the walls were going up, a gang of marauders came at night and threw burning torches into the enclosure. They did little damage because nothing was yet inside, but Lot was shocked and distraught.

Cheran was notified about the attack and came quickly to Lot's side.

"We will send guards to watch over the place day and night. This will not happen again."

"Abram warned me that this might happen and worse. How did these men know about the building? We are on the outer part of the city to be safer. Now it seems we are also in danger from those outside the city."

"It is likely they do not know the purpose of the building. They are just ignorant destroyers and my guards can make short work of them if they come back. It would be wise not to store any articles of value there. Just keep everything at Asya's. After they are used for services take them back to Asya's right away. Do not leave them at the temple unguarded, even half a day."

Lot was almost ready to give up but agreed to let Cheran place guards there. He could not let the few remaining elders at the city gate down if there was a way to continue on. It was their hope for something greater for times to come.

Meanwhile, the priests met with Lot at the temple and sometimes at the farm so they could instruct him in the ways of holy services and prayers.

A young man travelling from Elam heard about the work in Sodom, found the temple, and inquired if he might be accepted to be part of the work and worship. Lot recognized him. He was the young man he met in Elam who wanted Lot to help him escape. He was much younger than the elders in Elam, very quiet, and most interested in the Egyptians and their religions.

"Shemah! Is that really you? You survived! Tell me about your travels and how you found us."

"I have been traveling around this country and found Abram's people. They told me what you are doing and about the temple."

Lot was delighted to see him again and the priests welcomed him to participate in their studies. They made a place for him in the rooms of the temple that were nearly completed.

Shemah was thrilled to see all that Lot had done and was eager to become a teacher, a rabbi, and work in the temple. He had brothers and cousins who were coming to live with him to start a new life. This was exactly the life they had in mind and very much wanted to join the work as well. Lot assured him that they all would be welcome and there would be places in the temple for each of them to study and teach.

The brothers and cousins numbered twenty and were busy building adjacent dwelling places for themselves. As the temple grew, word spread throughout Sodom and a few curiosity seekers came at first. But then those who were serious about study and a new way of life stayed close by and formed a small congregation of students. Cheran instructed his guards to train them to defend themselves and the temple as it continued to grow.

They formed a small village on the outskirts of Sodom and created small textile industries to support themselves. Hadoram traded their goods for food from the farm. The farm families no longer had to buy expensive goods from passing caravans. They partnered with the temple to create their own market trade and with Asya to market their textiles. She was more than happy to help them with their designs and colors.

The temple idea grew and flourished beyond Lot's grandest dreams. Filled to overflowing with gratitude, Lot went into the hills behind the farm one evening and sat down on a hill overlooking the farm. He wanted to be alone with Abram's god, now his god, to count and give thanks for all of his blessings.

"My god, you have prospered me, given me a farm, wonderful people, family, and now young men ready to create worship in your temple. You rescued me from Elam, given me priests and soldiers, and most of all my uncle, Abram, who has loved me and treated me like a brother! I do not know what I have done to be so favored, but I humbly give thanks for it all."

It was late when Tebah went looking for Lot. He had seen him going into the hills and was worried something might have happened to him. He took a herding dog along to help him find Lot and scare away any wild animals.

"Father Lot, I do not wish to intrude, but we were concerned for your safety."

"Tebah, my son, you have always been a great blessing to me and to Anah. You are always welcome in my presence. Please come and sit for a moment and then we will return."

It was not lost on Tebah that Lot called him "my son." Lot had spoken to him at times about who would take over the farm when he and Hadoram were too old and passed on. He felt a warmth flow over him and made him more aware of a deep love for Lot that had been in his heart since childhood. As they walked back to the farm together they were companionably quiet and at peace.

Zehra demanded that Lot come home immediately. She sent servants to find him and they always returned with the same message.

"I will come when I am ready. I have several important things to attend to and you need not send any more terrified servants to fetch me."

She was incensed and screamed insults at the servants. She grabbed her flaxen robe and threw it around her shoulders.

"I will send more than you incompetent servants to get him! I will go myself!"

Though terrified, the servants knew how dangerous it was for Zehra to go alone. After she stormed out the door they shadowed her, keeping out of her sight. One servant stole away to find Cheran.

Cheran was about to head home when he saw a servant he recognized running toward him.

"You must come, master! The lady Zehra's home has been vandalized and many of her valuables were stolen. We found her bound and gagged in an outbuilding. She has gone out by herself to find Lot!"

"Alone?"

"Yes, but two men servants are following her staying in the shadows to keep her safe."

"More like to keep Sodom safe. She will tear the city down!"

Cheran knew Lot had returned and was at the temple. Probably that is where Zehra was headed.

She hated the temple and everything it stood for. She refused to set a foot into it, but stood outside and screamed for Lot. She was still outside of the temple fuming when Cheran arrived. He sent the servant home before she saw him so he would not be in trouble.

"Cheran! Where is that no good husband of mine?"

Cheran knew to ignore her insults.

"He has returned from the farm and gone with some builders to look at materials for the altar and coverings. Can I be of service, Zehra? Perhaps walk you back home?"

"Yes," spat Zehra and she strode away.

He broke into a trot to keep up with her.

"Zehra, what has happened?"

"My house was robbed, turned upside down, and I was attacked, bound and left in an outbuilding! Is that not enough?"

Cheran smiled and refrained from asking which outbuilding. He was shocked when they entered the house. It was literally upended as Zehra had said.

He sent the servant to his post for guards to go immediately to market and see if anyone was fencing jewelry there. He sent another servant to find Lot and bring others to help clean up the mess.

Zehra sat down and sobbed.

"Thank you, Cheran."

He brought her a glass of wine and wrapped a warm robe around her shoulders. It was the first and probably the last time she would appear human to him. He almost felt sorry for her, but knew better than to let that take hold. She had created her own misery and would viciously turn on him in an instant.

Lot came in a short time later, looked around, and called his builders to come on in. They began to set up furniture and pick up robes and statues from the floor.

"Be careful of those things!" shouted Zehra.

They ignored her and continued to follow Lot's instructions. They went through all the rooms putting things in order the best they could and left.

Lot sat down beside Zehra.

"Do you know who these robbers are? Did you recognize them?"

"They are from one of the caravans. When I refused to buy their goods they swore revenge."

"Exactly how did you refuse them? What did you say?"

"What do you mean? I will not buy inferior goods!"

"So you insulted them in front of all their customers! Zehra, even you should know better. They do not put up with insults, especially from a woman, and in front of their people! They retaliate!"

"I did nothing wrong!"

"Of course you did and look what you brought upon yourself! You will never learn."

Two of Cheran's guards came into the house and poured a bag of jewelry on the table before Zehra.

"Are these yours?"

Zehra's mouth dropped open. She lovingly ran her fingers through the jewelry.

"Yes, those are hers. Let's go."

Lot's disgust was growing by the second as he followed his builders to the door.

"You cannot leave! You need to stay and help. This is your house too, you know!"

Zehra was wide-eyed and rushed to block the door.

"Yes I can leave, Zehra. It is your house. The farm is mine. You have servants and you can clean the rest of this up yourself. Try not to terrify them so that they run away in the night."

# CHAPTER 21

∻∾∻∾∻∾∻∾∻∾∻∾∻∾∻∾∻∾∻∾∻∾∻∾∻∾∻∾∻∾∻∾∻∾∻∾∻∾∻∾∻∾

# DESTRUCTION

Gangs of men began to rob the caravans on the road before they came into Sodom. They slaughtered the people and stole the goods. They stole the caravan wagons, hauled everything away and hid it all in caves in the mountains.

Cheran's troops came into the city and followed the gangs to the next caravan. It became a war zone as the soldiers and gangs engaged in battles. As they killed gang members, more gangs arrived the next day and the days after that to take their place. Instead of gangs fighting each other, they were lining up to attack the caravans as Cheran's troops killed the gang ahead of them.

The caravans began to avoid Sodom and Gomorrah. Cheran sent messengers to call on other cities to send troops to protect the caravans while he went after the gangs in Sodom. The city of Ai remembered Cheran and were happy to post troops on the road to Sodom to protect the caravans.

Other marauders went after the wealthy homes in Sodom. Asya began moving her goods to the farm and Cheran set more guards at the house and around the market.

Lot brought in builders to secure Zehra's house with heavier doors, high walls, and a safe room on the roof. Soon people were prisoners in their own fortified houses, not daring to go out into the streets.

The priests from the temple came to Lot's house to warn him that the whole area was about to be destroyed, not by people but by the creation itself. They returned to the temple, closed it, and priests and students left immediately for Abram's camp.

Suddenly the earth became more unstable than usual. The roars and rumbles under the earth were heard and felt throughout the city. Gas fissures began to open in the streets and the gasses arose in foggy clouds. The ground rolled and pottery rattled on the shelves and fell to the floors.

Priests came again from the temple to warn Lot before they left.

"The city is about to be destroyed. Do you not feel the shaking? Take your family and servants and go to Abram immediately before it is too late!"

"But the earth always shakes here. There has been no danger or destruction all the years we have lived here."

Before they could speak again, a drunk and disorderly mob pounded on Lot's door and shouted for his guests to come out.

Lot was panicked.

"Go away! I have no guests!"

"We saw them come to your house! We will not go away! We want those men! Send them out and we will celebrate their visit!"

In desperation Lot gathered the servants to protect the door.

"Perhaps I will send someone else…tomorrow."

"No! Send them out! Send them out now!"

The shouting became louder and angrier. They began pounding on the door with rocks and poles, cracking the door. It broke and fell in.

As they stumbled over it to rush in, Lot's servants threw acidic sand from the salt sea into their faces blinding them and beat them with clubs until they crawled back out the door holding their heads. The servants quickly set the door back up, braced the breaks, and barred it again.

The earth continued to rumble and roll under their feet. There were loud cracking sounds in the house and booming sounds outside worse than thunder.

"Lot, you must go now!"

Immediately they turned and fled out the back way, through the streets and alleys toward the mountains.

Lot sent the servants to load wagons with their household goods and food, and prepared to leave for Abram's valley in the mountains.

Asya and Anah's children were across town at a birthday celebration. Their husbands had gone to the city council to assess the dangers. The sisters had been looking at the latest fabrics and purchases in their mother's collection that the merchants had delivered to Zchra's house. Zehra now made her selections at home. They reveled in the exotic silks from far away. The colors were luminous and the perfumes were heavenly.

They became alarmed at the yells of the men from the streets. Then the floors began to shake and lift. Everything began tumbling to the floor. They could hardly stand up.

Lot burst into the room.

"Come, we must leave for Abram's in the mountains immediately. There is no time!"

Asya shouted over the increasing noise of the rumbling earth.

"But our families!"

"Cheran and Tebah will keep them safe. Come! We must go!"

They gathered clothing and Zehra's silks and stuffed them into the merchant's cloth bags. Servants rushed in to gather them and carry them out to the wagons that were already filled with food and utensils. The skittish animals were brought from the stable out back, harnesses flung onto their backs and stable boys hitching them to the wagons.

Fissures in the ground were already opening up throughout the city. Gasses fumed up along the streets catching the fire from oil lamps and spreading with terrifying speed. More fire spewed forth from cracks in earth. Fire and ash began to rain down from the sky. There was no way to get to Abram's valley now.

The heat rose and intensified, trapped between the mountains that lined the valley to the east and west, and by the pressure of the atmosphere at sea level a thousand or more feet above the city. Larger fires sprang up creating one gigantic inferno. Tornado like winds formed columns of fire that shot up hundreds of feet and ash rained back down from the sky, setting the whole city on fire.

Lot dragged a struggling Zehra and his stumbling daughters from the house. The servants finished loading wagons with household goods and they all made a run for it to the south. The shaking nearly upset a wagon.

"We will go east to Zoar," shouted Lot."

Others from Sodom were rushing in that same direction. Some people from Gomorrah and Admah were coming down from the north from their burning cities and were fleeing in that direction as well.

Chaos erupted. People trampled each other and wagons overturned, spilling goods on the ground.

Asya and Anah kept looking at the crowds hoping to see Cheran, Tebah, Dishon, Joktan, and Atarah. And where was Hannah?

"They must be here somewhere. Surely Cheran and Tebah will get the families out!"

Despite Lot's pleading they left the wagons to search, but no one had seen them. They called their names over and over until the smoke choked their throats and voices. They rushed back through the pushing and fear crazed crowds to the wagons sobbing and gasping, nearly collapsing.

The way was becoming more difficult. Falling stones and debris were littering the streets. The smoke was becoming almost too thick to see through, but Lot pulled them forward. He had an escape route in mind.

Moving around the tip of the sea, the smoke thinned a little and travel was easier. They struggled on until at last the edge of the city of Zoar was in sight.

Zehra was staggering, enraged that Lot forced them to leave Sodom. "You cannot force me to leave! I am going back!"

She turned and ran back toward Sodom. Lot ran after her and shouted for her to stop. But she ran wildly on until the erupting gasses exploded, enveloping her, and she disappeared into the vapors and flames. Lot fell backward shocked and stunned.

Many others were also running back toward the city hoping to find families and retrieve their belongings. They, too, disappeared and were incinerated in the growing holocaust.

Lot could see that Zoar was becoming more dangerous by the minute. The stampeding crowds were headed that way. The residents were battling to keep them out, trying to protect their city.

With his wife gone and his daughters screaming in horror that their families were nowhere to be found, Lot dragged them back to the wagons and altered his route to leave Zoar.

There was only one thing to do. Take his daughters and their servants high up into the eastern mountain range. They turned to the east across the north end of Zoar, avoiding the crush of desperate and terrified people coming into the south and west sides of the city.

Their wagon wheels crashed and crunched over debris that was spilling onto the ground from the air. The clouds of burning debris were roiling over the sea toward Zoar.

They covered their heads with rugs to protect them from the fiery debris, while the servants pulled robes and hoods tight, and struggled with the terrified animals pulling the wagons.

Lot kept his calm as he walked alongside the leading servants, stumbling and guiding them to the clearer streets that began to appear through the swirling smoke. At last the buildings became fewer, the frenzied crowds were behind them, and the foot hills lay ahead.

They followed pathways that carried them to higher plateaus where they could uncover themselves and look back over the incredible holocaust. Exhausted and dazed Lot urged them onward and upward.

Moving the wagons under a narrow overhang of rock, he sent two servants to search the many caves above for a suitable place to stop and take cover. Many caves were too shallow or too small. Some had no flat floor, and some were filled with boulders and crevices. It was harder and harder to make progress as the path steepened.

Finally they saw the shadow of an opening or entrance higher up. The servants climbed up to see it. It was suitable, but the way up was difficult. The servants motioned Lot to bring the wagons as close as possible. Everyone including Asya and Anah helped to throw stones out of the way of the wagon wheels. The servants levered boulders loose and pushed them down the cliffs to widen the path.

They spent nights in the wagons and the servants under the wagons, covered with rugs and tapestries to keep warm. In the mornings they would pick up bags of household goods and haul them up to the cave. The treks to the cave took a few days to complete because of the difficulty of the climb.

They looked out over the valley hoping to see the smoke clear, but it was the same every day. Only smoke and blackness were visible. Even the buildings in Zoar were covered in black soot. It seemed as if their whole world were completely destroyed. Nothing left but ashes.

Asya sat down drained. Anah sobbed and wrapped her arms around her sister.

"Our families are surely gone, perhaps died in Sodom without a chance to get out!"

It was a horrible thought and Asya would not consider it. She refused to give up.

"Suppose they all got out! They were at the other end of the city. We do not know what happened there."

"Even if they did get out, how will they find us, Asya? They might even think we are dead!"

"If they did escape, they will not stop until they find us, we can be sure of that. We will send messages with everyone who passes this way. We escaped once from captivity in Elam and we will survive this, too."

Asya was determined as ever.

"From what we saw in Zoar, many people escaped. I guess there is still hope..."

Anah's voice was not filled with certainty, but she was willing to follow Asya's lead.

They climbed out of the wagon and lifted more bundles to carry to the cave. Their fingers and knees were raw from scrambling to the cave entrance. The smoke still coated their throats causing them to cough constantly.

Lot was continually out of breath and gasping, stopping often. The servants begged him to rest and let them do the lifting and climbing. They helped him up to the cave where he sat down against some bundles. Asya brought him a flask of wine to ease his cough and pain.

The servants worked quickly to get everything into the cave and to arrange living quarters for everyone as best they could. They wanted to give Lot a comfortable place to lie down and rest. He was shivering, coughing violently and spitting a bit of blood.

They helped him to the bed prepared for him and covered him. Anah sat by him throughout the night until his coughing quieted and he slept. She finally dosed off before dawn, dreaming of the life on the farm, the joy and love, the good times...

# CHAPTER 22

❖⬦❖⬦❖⬦❖⬦❖⬦❖⬦❖⬦❖⬦❖⬦❖⬦❖⬦❖⬦❖⬦❖⬦❖⬦❖⬦❖⬦❖

# THE CAVE

With all the belongings brought up to the cave, one of the servants guarded the entrance, ready to protect the family and even kill anyone who might be threatening harm. The wafting fumes from Sodom and Gomorrah still choked them at times, but there would hopefully be cool clear air in the recesses of the cave.

Carefully the servants, Asya, and Anah picked their way back through the darkness, over the stones and sandy floor, and feeling their way along the rough walls of the cave until the air was cooler, clear and breathable. The damp walls at the back told them that somewhere above there was water. Two servants went up above the cave immediately to look for the source.

They lit small lamps to assess their living surroundings, finding that the cave was much more spacious that they had first thought. There was room for everything from the wagons to be arranged in niches in the walls. The servants wrapped and stored the food, wine, figs, fruit, bread and dried fish, in the coolest place in the farthest reach of the cave. They laid out rugs and pillows for the family's comfort and made a small oven for cooking out of stones in a shallow cave a little higher up but close by.

The servants who untethered the animals led them higher up to small patches of grass in a pass where they could graze. A stray herding dog came bounding up to them, making friendly yips and wagging its tail. They patted its head and pointed it to the animals hoping it would guard them. The lonely dog was happy to be with people and joyfully ran to do his herding job. There were stray sheep in the area as well, so the dog herded them in with the pack animals.

A very small stream ran through the area not too far away, the one that probably dampened the walls of the cave. They built a small race to direct some of the water into jars they could carry to the cave until they could tap the water dampening the cave walls.

With everything in place there was nothing to do but wait. Asya and Anah waited impatiently and hoped that somehow their families escaped and would find them. Day after day passed slowly and nothing changed.

The smoke and gasses continued to hang over the destroyed cities and from time to time the stench wafted past the entrance to their cave, reminding them of all that was lost. There was no going back to look for anyone or anything. Nothing was there.

Asya was not content to just sit too much longer. She abruptly stood and shading her eyes, squinted up at the higher elevations.

"I am going to explore the pass and what else is above us. Anah, will you come with me?"

Anah was startled out of her thoughts. She was not the adventurous type, but there was nothing else to do. She took a deep breath and gathered her courage.

"Yes, I will go with you."

A servant was afraid for their safety.

"Please, my ladies, do not go alone. There might be great dangers! Wild animals and cliffs! Please, allow me to accompany you."

Asya thought for a few minutes.

"Thank you, Uriah, but we will be all right. I prefer that you stay here with our father and see to his needs and take care of the cave and our animals in the pasture."

He bowed slightly and hurried to the cave of the oven. He brought back knives for them to carry, and small bundles of food. They put the food in a fold of their robes and looked quizzically at the servant as they examined the knives.

"You will need these weapons, my ladies. There may be wild animals and you may need to kill them for food."

"Thank you, Uriah. You have always been a blessing to us."

Sometimes they were away for several days. Asya killed small game and Anah skinned and cooked it over a fire pit.

"What do people do who have lost everything? When we were captives there were people around us and cities close by. But here we are...alone..."

"We keep up hope, Anah, and continue to survive until something happens to change things."

"But what if it takes forever? What if nothing does change and we live out our lives in a cave with no one? No husbands and families?"

Anah couldn't stop the tears that seemed to come on their own without her permission.

Asya picked at her food and gazed at the far mountains.

"There are no 'what if's' and there is only today, Anah. We may have tomorrow and tomorrow may bring something. That is what we can do and hope for. It does not help to think this will be our lives forever."

Anah dried her tears and reached for a crust of bread.

"Well, our days may not be so empty because we have our memories. Perhaps we could tell each other stories about our past and our family's past. We can share what we know about them, how we grew up, and came to be ourselves now. I am sure we have some different memories about the same things."

"Anah! I did not know you were such a deep thinker!"

"See, there it is! Something you did not know about me already! I know you did not think I had a wise mind, but I did and I do. I just never talked about these things much. I did not think anyone would care to listen. Girls are not supposed to be able to think!"

Asya got an impish grin on her face.

"Well, let me tell you how our mother ended up in the Elam palace dungeon…"

They came back to the cave to find Lot only slightly better. He coughed a little less, but he was weak and tired, still short of breath and did not move beyond the cave. It distressed him to see the ruined valley below. It always brought tears to his eyes so he refrained from looking down at it.

"My beautiful farm is gone. All of our work destroyed. Did our people from the farm escape? I pray they did."

The servants were settled in and seemed to enjoy the peaceful mountain life in contrast to noisy clangorous Sodom. Sodom was all they had ever known. They thought the whole world was like that. This was a completely new experience for them. Now they could wander about without fear of being attacked.

They made a living area for themselves in the kitchen cave where they would not disturb Lot with their chatter. One servant always slept near Lot when the daughters were away in case he awakened in distress during the night.

After several weeks Asya noticed that there were some people moving around below them in the foothills and beyond in the distance.

"They must be some of the survivors! I wonder if we know them."

Excitedly Asya and Anah picked their way down the path they had cleared to reach the cave, to take a closer look. Anah was suddenly skeptical.

"They could be thieves or someone desperate. How will we know if they are friendly? They could be from the gangs in Sodom."

Asya checked the knife in the fold of her robe to be sure it was handy.

"You may be right! Better we meet them down there than wait until they come up and find our cave."

A couple who were occupying a space under an overhang were startled to see Asya and Anah approaching. The woman came forward a few steps and called out to them.

"If you are coming to steal from us, we have nothing."

"We are not coming to steal. I guess we are neighbors. I am Asya and my sister Anah. We are alone up on the mountain ridge in a cave with our father and some servants. We are so happy to see you! Are you from Sodom? Are there others who survived?"

"We are from Gomorrah. We were coming to Sodom to visit relatives when the tremors began and then the fires. We were fortunate to have a good supply of food with us and some robes, but that is all we have. I am Zoah and this is my husband, Ham. Please come and sit with us. We have been ill from the smoke and have not moved about much, but we are a little better now."

"Our father, Lot, is quite ill and does not seem to be recovering. Probably from the smoke and gasses. There is no physician among us."

They chatted companionably until the evening. Asya and Anah promised to return with grains for bread and other foods, and made their way up to the cave just before dark.

"You see, Anah? Now, what do you suppose will tomorrow bring? We have Hope!"

"Asya, how do you keep yourself uplifted and a smile on your face, even when we look out at the valley? It takes so much work for me to stay that way, even for half a day."

"When I look out, I do not see the valley. I see Cheran coming for me, laughing and taking me in his arms. The more I see that in my mind, the more certain I am that it will happen and soon."

The next several months brought more people who escaped the devastation and soon there was a small community gathered in the foothills below their cave. Lot was still too weak and ill to climb down to meet them, but he enjoyed sitting in the mouth of the cave and watching them go about their tasks.

Asya and Anah became proficient hunters and brought the some of the game they killed down to a grateful community. Others went out with them to hunt as well. They found an old deserted vineyard and were able to replenish their supply of wine with the now wild grapes. Everyone shared what they had and sent bread and wishes for his recovery up to Lot.

No one spoke of the friends and family they lost. They kept their eyes turned to the future and as Asya often said, hope.

Asya and Anah shared one fervent hope, that their husbands and children were somewhere still alive and thinking about them, too. Every day they became more certain of this. Hope had turned into a sense of knowing and anticipation.

Zoah and Ham caught their enthusiasm.

"I am sure they are! From what you have told us about them, they are survivors. We hold on to hope but we do not dwell upon the past. Everything now is a gift that we gratefully accept! Think about their return to you as a gift yet to come."

# CHAPTER 23

❖❖❖❖❖❖❖❖❖❖❖❖❖❖❖❖❖❖❖❖❖❖❖❖❖❖❖❖❖❖❖❖❖❖❖❖

# THE SEARCH

Cheran and Tebah and their families fled with the king to the western mountains above the city. Tebah wanted to search for Asya and Anah, but Cheran shouted over the roar.

"There is no time! Lot will take care of them! Run!"

They threw rugs over their heads as they ran to escape the explosions and the flaming pieces falling from the sky. Dishon and Joktan grabbed the hands of people who were stumbling and pulled them along. Atarah carried an infant that was thrust into her arms by its mother before she fell dead.

Their feet were blistering and their throats were raw. They scrambled into the recesses of mountain caves and stopped momentarily to catch their breath. The explosions and heat were rising behind them.

They frantically continued climbing, fingers raw, and the heat scorching their backs, until they came to the top of the ridge. They ran stumbling and tripping down the other side, away from the holocaust to cooler air and safety. They lay panting on the cooler ground coughing, catching their breath and checking on each other for wounds or broken bones. Thankfully, they were all well enough to continue.

Cheran and King Bera knew the way to Abram's camp. They had made a similar harrowing escape years after the attack of the northern kings. It took three days to get there carrying the injured. Atarah, still carrying the baby, ran on ahead to call for help. She fell into the arms of a guard hardly able to speak until she could catch her breath.

The men in the camp rushed to meet the survivors and carried the injured back to the camp. The women met them, took the crying baby from Atarah, and began tending to everyone's scrapes and burns.

The guard called for Abram and helped Atarah into the camp. The tale she told was a shocking nightmare. It was hard for them to picture in their minds that the entire city was blowing up and burning down, much less that most of the population burned up with it.

Abram and Sarai rushed to them, alarmed and horrified at the report from Atarah and Cheran.

"Sodom and Gomorrah are destroyed, and we do not know how many other cities as well! Maybe Admah and Zoar were far enough away to be saved from the worst of it."

"We do not know about Lot, Zehra, Asya, and Anah. Some people were running in the direction of Zoar on the other side of the sea..."

"We were on the west side of the city and they were at Zehra's. So we could not get to them to know what happened or where they went. God of Abram! I hope they all got out and we will be able to find them!"

Tebah was devastated at the thought of losing them.

"We have survived invasions and all manner of evil, but this is beyond endurance. Everything was fire and explosions all around us. I wanted to find them, but..."

Then Hannah appeared from the far end of the camp. She ran and threw her arms around Tebah, shocked to hear about the destruction of Sodom. She reached for Atarah and they held each other tight.

"Everyone at the farm escaped up into the hills and are all safe here, father Tebah. Hadoram saved us all. Where are mother and aunt Asya? Are they with you? Where is Grandfather Lot?"

She looked wildly around.

"Asya and Anah were not with us at the celebration, but home at Lot and Zehra's. We do not know how people on that side of the city fared. We could not even look for them! The place was blowing up and catching fire all around us."

Tebah was still drying his tears of joy at seeing Hannah safe. Cheran put an arm around him.

"I wanted to save them, but…"

"You know there was no time, Tebah! We must trust that they found a way out and we will go soon to search for them. They may have gone to Zoar with others who escaped.

"We cannot go near Sodom. It is too dangerous, like a boiling pot. It is probably still burning and will be for months. But we can go to all the places around it where the people who got out are encamped. Take heart, Tebah. They are brave and resourceful and we can trust that."

All was quiet in Abram's camp that night, but everyone was awake with their own images of the fires and fears of what they might or might not find. Even though they were eager to find their families, they were forced to rest for a few weeks. Their breathing was becoming more normal, their coughing from inhaling the smoke eased, and most of their wounds were shallow and healing.

Eventually Cheran, Tebah, and King Bera sat down with Abram and made plans to leave soon for Jericho where they could cross the river and travel down the east side of the valley.

Abram called his able bodied men together and organized a small caravan of those who were free of responsibilities to go. Most stayed to carry on the work of the camp and care for the families. Cheran's sons,

Dishon and Joktan, daughter Atarah, and niece Hannah were also going. They quickly packed supplies to carry and would take just a few pack animals so they could travel faster.

"But sire, you are the king and should not risk the travel to these dangerous places. We almost lost you once!"

"Cheran, my trusted aide, I am no longer a king. My city is destroyed and my people are scattered or dead. You and I have clawed our way through these mountains more than once, and I cannot sit here and wait, useless and growing old!"

Cheran remembered those times and felt a little foolish. He agreed reluctantly.

"I will be by your side as always, my lord."

They left Abram's camp and pressed on down to Jericho to cross over the Jordan.

They were told bits of stories from travelers and stragglers from Admah and the destroyed cities who they met along their way. Their experiences were harrowing, full of terror and loss. They were hollow-eyed and in shock, and just trudged on. None of them offered a shred of hope that anyone else could have survived.

The merchants in the Jericho market place were shocked to hear what happened to Sodom and Gomorrah.

"There were strong tremors here in Jericho as well, but nothing was destroyed by them. Are you saying that Sodom and Gomorrah went up in explosions and flames? Entire cities are gone?"

Cheran winced at the question. He was still experiencing the emotional pain remembering the explosions and the heat on his back as they ran.

"Sadly they are completely gone my friend. Only black ash remains. We are hoping to find our wives, their father, and our servants alive somewhere on the east side of the sea.

"There are five of us who escaped and bought the news. Most of the people died unable to get out in time. We are going to the area around it to see if any of our family members and, perhaps others, escaped to

Zoar and could be there or encamped somewhere in the mountains near Zoar."

With some information offered by merchants and sketchy maps about the caravan route on the east side of the river, Abram's little caravan set out moving south toward Zoar. The going was not difficult until the major caravan route abruptly turned east taking them too far away from the river and the sea. They left the caravan route and made an arduous climb up through a pass and downward toward the water's edge.

They traveled as close to the river and Salt Sea as possible. Some of the paths dwindled to mere goat paths going through huge rocky formations, and then widened out again through the foothills and down into flatter land.

They came upon remnants of old deserted camps and more recent camps where people were injured or sick and dying. Atarah and Hannah attended to some of them, but in most cases they could be of little or no help other to give them water and bread. People were ill from the gasses and smoke and needed only to rest in the fresh air, hopefully to recover.

Strange dark poisonous looking clouds hung over the sea and to the south and west. The smell of smoke and stench of the destruction began to reach their nostrils and irritated their eyes. They drew their face coverings closer.

Coming nearer to Zoar the population in the hills and caves increased. There were more plentiful signs of life appearing in the foothills. People peered curiously at them and turned away.

Encouraged Cheran and Tebah went on ahead calling the names, Asya, Anah, and Lot! The hills would echo back their shouts, but no human response came as yet.

They began to scramble up to the caves to look for them. People they found pointed them on toward more caves higher up, but no one they met knew any names of the survivors.

Signs of devastation became more widespread and those who escaped were coughing and barely surviving. Atarah and Hannah continued to help the people along the shoreline, bringing water, bread, wraps, crutches Joktan made from scrub trees, and a little hope.

When Asya and Anah returned from a hunting trip, the servants told them that they heard people down below shouting from time to time.

"Yes, men were shouting but we could not understand what they were shouting or see who it was. Too many echoes. We kept watching but we saw no one."

High in the mountain foothills over Zoar, Cheran heard a response to his call. He began to scramble up the cliff to a plateau where he saw Asya coming toward him. She fell into his arms sobbing and laughing at the same time.

"We did not know if you were alive! And Dishon, Joktan, and Atarah?"

"All alive. Hannah as well. She was visiting in Abram's camp when it happened. Tebah! They are alive! Lot, Anah, and my Asya! Up here! Up here!"

Joy filled Abram as he settled the small caravan below and they all followed the path that was created when Lot and his servants found the cave. The reunion was full of joy and tears. They spent weeks together recounting their stories. The most frightening story was about Zehra and her violent death.

"We could not find her remains to bury them, so we designated a pillar of salt above the sea as her marker. You can see it from here with one of her bright scarves tied around it."

King Bera stood on a high cliff and shading his eyes, looked sadly toward Sodom. Below him Zoar was black but the buildings were still standing and clearly visible. The edge of Sodom in the distance was only a thin horizontal black line barely discernable.

"There is no need for me to go further toward the city. There is nothing to find except ash."

He turned and slowly climbed back down to Lot's cave a little below.

Lot began to cough and spit blood. Abram was alarmed.

"Lot, my brother, you are not well!"

Lot choked out that it was the ash and gasses he inhaled as they escaped to Zoar and then escaped from Zoar as well.

"I am a little better and with some rest I should be well."

Abram was doubtful. Lot was thin and his face pale. He could not stand without a crutch or help from the servants. His coughing fits through the nights disturbed his sleep. He ate little. This was not the stocky robust man Abram knew, but a mere shadow of himself, hardly recognizable.

"I will stay with you, my brother. A messenger I sent will let everyone in my valley know you all have survived. They will be overjoyed."

"Tell Sarai that I miss her. She was always a true friend and sister."

"I will tell her. Please rest now."

Lot smiled weakly as he laid back on his thin bed, coughed, and sank into a slumber.

# CHAPTER 24

❖❖❖❖❖❖❖❖❖❖❖❖❖❖❖❖❖❖❖❖❖❖❖❖❖❖❖❖❖❖❖

# LOT'S PASSING

The hardships of the escape had taken their toll. His body was wasting away. His daughters kept him wrapped in robes and slept beside him to keep him warm, but his shivering did not stop even when he slept. Lot was not recovering.

He was coughing and gasping for air. His lungs were poisoned and weak. His wracking coughing echoed through the cave day and night. His mind often became confused from the lack of oxygen. He thought he was still on the farm and he called for Hadoram to help him lift a tree off his chest.

He was dying.

Abram stayed close to him, taking advantage of every moment that Lot was lucid.

"Lot, do you believe in some kind of life after death?"

"Oh, God of All, no! Not if it means I would have to spend eternity with Zehra. One lifetime with her was enough!"

They had many good laughs which brought on spasms of Lot's coughing.

Sometimes his mind was clear and they talked about all their adventures from Haran until now. They reminisced over the invasion, capture and escape. The rebuilding of their lives seemingly many times over, from Ur to Hebron, Canaan to Egypt, and back to Canaan again.

"I will miss seeing Sarai again. I wish she could have come with you. Abram, do you still believe in God's promise of a child, a nation, for you and Sarai?"

"I thought Sarai had nearly given up, but now we have a child, Isaac. We no longer talk about a nation. I keep that to myself and in my prayers knowing that God of All will reveal everything in time, but perhaps not in my time."

"Abram, God's promise seemed so impossible to me. It is hard to understand. I have figured out farming, building, and business, but I have not figured out God. Perhaps we can never understand God."

Soon Lot mostly slept and no longer tried to speak. Abram and the family took turns sitting by him. Abram held Lot as he had held Terah in his arms when Lot took his last few rasping breaths. Family and servants gathered around him as his coughing eased and then his breathing stopped, and he was gone.

Abram and his servants prepared to carry his body home to his camp to the hills around the plain of Hebron, where they settled when they came out of Egypt so many years ago. The caravan was again loaded and King Bera accompanied Abram and the soldiers on the sad journey back to Jericho, then to Ai and home.

Cheran, Asya, Tebah, and Anah, their sons and daughters all stayed in the cave. They spent months discerning their next steps and their future. Their future did not seem to be with Abram's people. They needed to recreate their own home and determine where it would be.

Daily Dishon, Joktan, Atarah and Hannah made their way to the higher plains where there was grazing and water. The animals were lodged in corrals and shaded in small shelters. The lonely herding dog leaped for joy at their arrival, but he stayed on the job when they moved on.

They scouted the land beyond the ridges and through the passes of the mountains. One day they came through a pass and looked down upon the continuing trade route they had left to follow the shore of the Salt Sea. It extended long distances to the north and south before it disappeared into mountains.

Joktan spotted a large caravan slowly making its way from the north on the caravan road.

"We should go down to meet them! If they are friendly, perhaps they can tell us more about the land here in the east."

They made their way down to the caravan and Dishon inquired about the merchants and leader, that they might speak with them.

"We are from the city of Sodom, which is now completely destroyed. It blew up in earthquakes and fires. There is nothing left. Nothing at all. This is my brother Joktan, my sister Atarah, and our cousin Hannah."

Dishon was directed to the leader and guide of the combined caravans.

"I am Adnan. Come with us and be welcome. We will camp a short distance from here. We wish to know all that has happened to Sodom. This is very sad news. And are the cities of Gomorrah and Zoar also damaged?"

They were given tents in which to rest and food. It seemed that everyone in the caravan wanted to know about Sodom. They spent a few days describing the destruction and the survivors now living in the caves along the shore of the Salt Sea.

They answered the questions as well as they could and explained that there was no time to stop for anything, just get away into the hills and as far as possible from the explosions and fires.

"So you got away from the destruction and fires with only the clothes on your backs?"

"Yes and barely that. The fire was so close behind us that they were nearly burned right off our backs. We escaped to the west to the camp of Abram in the upper valleys of the plain of Hebron. But our grandfather and mothers escaped to the east with a wagon or two of goods. They went through Zoar which nearly caught fire itself. Many escapees were also running toward Zoar and creating chaos. Lot decided to move on into the foothills and they found a cave in the side of the mountains in which to dwell. There are others who have gathered there down in the foothills, all survivors."

"Abram and Hebron! Yes! We know him and that place! Abram is a great man and we very much admire him. He is a friend of Melchizedek, the Holy and Blessed One. We will give you goods and the pack animals to carry everything back to your caves."

"But we have almost nothing to trade."

"We will see Abram when we go to Ai and Bethel. He will compensate us if we so desire. But do not be concerned about that now. Let us help to get your community begun again. It would be good if you could settle along this trade route where you can thrive and grow."

Amazed, Joktan and Dishon bowed low to these generous people.

"We will settle here as you suggest. What is this place called?"

"Some call it Moab. It means 'seed of the father, water of the water flowing from the father.' This is a good omen. Settle a little farther to the north from here. There is a valley where you will find fertile land and water. There is room for the whole community of survivors if they will come with you. You can build, prosper, and trade again."

They graciously accepted the gifts, took their leave kissing cheeks and letting tears flow, and went north to find the place that was recommended. There was, indeed, a large green valley, water and grasses, far enough off the caravan route so it was not immediately exposed to travelers.

Taking the pack animals and gifts, they turned back to cross the mountain passes and ridges to the cave at the Salt Sea, excited to share the news.

"Moab is a new land with a valley waiting for us to settle there. We can begin again! We will help each other to rebuild our lives. Caravans will come by for trade and we will be a community that is alive and thriving again."

Asya laughed and hugged them all. "Yes, we are truly beginning again. Anah and I are both with child!"

Cheran and Tebah stopped in their tracks and their mouths dropped open.

"How can this be?" exclaimed Tebah. "Well, I mean this is unexpected is it not?"

Anah hugged him. "We are without the midwives who provided us with herbs to help avoid child bearing."

Asya had been dismayed at being with child living out in the caves away from a city, but Anah was thrilled.

"Well what could we expect with two hungry husbands returning from exile? We will be all right. We will help each other. It will be nice to have babies in the family again. Lord knows Atarah and Hannah have other plans for their lives that do not include babies."

Asya and Anah busied themselves making infant clothing and preparing for two babies. Atarah and Hannah stayed a little closer to them until the time came for their deliveries. The months went by slowly as they rested and made plans for the future in the valley of Moab.

Joktan and Dishon were making plans about how to move everything into the valley off the caravan route, and helping some of the community in the foothills below to move with them if they so desired. It seemed that all the survivors were thrilled to see a new life beginning for them too. They hurried to pack what little they had into the cloth bags that Asya gave them.

They began the long arduous trek over the mountains and into the valley. Some traveled with packs on their backs and weaker people were on the backs of the animals. Their eyes widened with amazement as they first glimpsed the beauty of the valley, so different from the foothills of the Salt Sea.

A son was born to Asya and Cheran. They decided to name him Moab after the new land and the new lives they were ready to embark upon. Then a few weeks later a son, Ammon, was born to Anah and Tebah.

"Hope, Anah! Look what it has brought to us! New life, new homes, new families, and our second family of children!"

"I am happy that you are no longer upset about having another child, but thrilled with our new babies!"

"When I look into those little faces, how could I be anything but overjoyed? They are so sweet and lovable. I have almost forgotten what that was like."

Cheran and Tebah were like brothers, much like Abram and Lot. They walked the hills together talking about a whole new world that was dawning around them. They thought about Abram's and Lot's God of All that presumably had brought them this far. Tebah was deep in thought about it all.

"Perhaps we are part of the new nation promised to Abram. But still we are not Abram's children. Was that promise not made to Abram that he would create a new nation?"

"The promise, as I remember being told, was that God would make of him a great nation. How could Abram do that by himself? He and Sarai alone? We are his kin, Lot being Abram's nephew."

He and Cheran sat silent for a long time, looking out over the valley, the coming new world they could see from their high perch and in their minds.

"Far be it from us to discern the workings of creation, even the God of All. I am just grateful for all that I have. The farm may be gone, but life has always moved forward and I am sure it will continue in the new valley."

"Moab," whispered Cheran. "A new beginning."

"A new beginning," echoed Tebah.

Servants worked for several days to repair the wagons that were battered by the rocky paths and finally to load the last of their household goods. Most were happy to be leaving this cave of sadness, the caves they were forced to live in after the destruction of their beloved homes, and the cave where Lot died.

They brought the animals down that were still in the high pastures to pull the wagons to the new land. The community on the foothills was completely cleared of people and goods. Even the feeble and disabled felt enlivened and wanted to join in the adventure and the new life in the valley.

Asya, Anah, and the babies were nearly the last to leave. They stood on a bluff and took a long look over the Salt Sea and to the south where Sodom had been. They missed their father, Lot, terribly.

They checked around the cave for the last time. Tears came to their eyes as they joined the last of the community leaving what had been a world of pain, and going forward to the wonderful future that awaited them.

Little by little the community was established. It began to grow and flourish, and they called it Moab, after the Valley of Moab. They were the first Moabites, the beginning of the tribe of Moab.

# CHAPTER 25

~~~~~~~~~~~~~~~~~~~~~~~~~~~~~~~~~~~~~~~~~~~~~~~~~~~~~~~~~~~~

# SARAH AND ABRAHAM

It was a perfect time to send a messenger to take the news to Sarai and Abram about the new place in the valley of Moab. Atarah and Hannah enthusiastically volunteered for the trip, and Atarah spoke up immediately.

"We have done all we can do here in the valley and we long to go back to our childhood home and share all the good news. I want to stop in Ai and Bethel and brag that it was my mother rode there on a horse!"

Asya gasped, "Oh, no!"

And Cheran laughed.

Hannah was thrilled!

"Yes! What fun! And I would like to see all those who survived from the farm again. We have so much to talk about since your escape from Elam and the destruction of Sodom and Gomorrah. I cannot wait to hear their stories."

Cheran was shocked that they were so eager to go without a thought for their safety.

"You surely will not travel alone!"

Always astonished at the strength of their daughters, Asya and Anah reluctantly agreed that they should go and began gathering supplies for their journey.

Anah and Asya smiled at each other.

"We always thought they should have been boys, but they seem to be able to overcome any frailties women are thought to have."

Dishon and Joktan arrived in the middle of the conversation and announced they would go as well. Cheran drew a deep breath of relief that the girls would not be going by themselves.

Asya and Anah laughed at the looks on the father's faces.

Asya hugged him. "Do not be surprised, father Cheran, if it is the girls who actually protect the boys. It will be a contest to see who can slaughter the enemy first!"

When the four arrived in Jericho, they sought out their families' fellow travelers from Haran so long ago. Joshua and Rebecca were still there in their ancestral home. Their daughters, Lilia and Rachel, were married and living across the Jordan. Their son Jared was a city official of Jericho, still unmarried and quite wealthy.

They were delighted to welcome Asya and Anah's children into their homes. They spent many evenings on the roof of the house together sharing watered wine, bread, and fruit. They loved hearing each other's stories of all that had happened to the families since they left Haran and then Egypt.

Joshua, Rebecca, and Jared decided to accompany the four to Abram's valley, eager to see their old friends again. Jared took time away from his duties to accompany them since Joshua and Rebecca were getting on in years and would welcome his assistance.

They traveled to Ai and Bethel and were greeted joyously by those who knew them and some who did not, but had heard the stories. They spent the evenings there sharing the stories of Abram's rescue of Lot and the escape of Asya on horseback from Elam.

Atarah was a little wide-eyed. She had not heard all of the details of her mother's escape.

"Please tell me more! I only know that she stole a horse and galloped out of the closing city gate into the night. And she always says that I am the wild one! How many times did you say she fell off the horse?"

Everyone laughed and passed the wine around again continuing the merriment and stories that lasted late into the nights.

Though a little sleepy from the late nights, they set out early in the morning for Abram's camp before the heat became unbearable.

Abram and Sarai welcomed them all with shouts of joy. There were tears and embraces for Joshua, Rebecca, and Jared as well.

"I cannot believe you are all here! Come and refresh yourselves. You can bathe and the servants will bring you bread and wine and fresh tunics. Then rest and we will share a meal."

Abram called a gathering to come and celebrate their return. A huge feast was set out by the servants and a few musicians played and sang.

Atarah could hardly contain her excitement to tell the news.

"Mother Asya and Aunt Anah will come when their babies are ready to travel in a few years. Their names are Moab and Ammon. Moab is my brother and was named after the valley of their new home."

Abram's mouth dropped open in surprise.

"Atarah, you are just swimming in brothers! How will you cope?"

"Yes, I am, and I can still take them all down! One at a time of course. Ask Cheran and Tebah! And now Hannah has a brother too, Ammon. We will be old when those two are grown up but it is fine! We love them."

There was a din of conversation at the meal buzzing all around the tables. Young children of the residents who came from the farm, and of Abram's people and servants, were running around the grounds shrieking with laughter and the sheep dogs were jumping and yelping in the excitement.

After the meal, small groups of people eventually drifted away to talk, and left Abram and Sarai's family to be alone together.

Atarah and Hannah had heard their grandmother's stories about the hated Sarai, but they found Sarai to be beautiful and fascinating, and they immediately fell in love with her.

"Oh, your grandmother and I were very young and traveling through mountains and deserts, rough roads, blighted towns, dusty fields and past dry streams all the way to Egypt.

"It was very hard for everyone, but Zehra was a social butterfly, not accustomed to such hardships. She was forced by her father, Bethuel, into the marriage to Lot. She had made her family's lives very difficult in Haran with her flirtatious ways in the market place. She was becoming a disgrace to her family.

"She was pretty and beguiling, and Lot so wanted to marry her, not seeing the impossible challenges she would encounter, living in tents and traveling caravan routes through mountains and deserts. I fear I was quite hard on her, but we were all faced with survival every step of the way."

Sarai wept when she heard of Zehra's horrible demise.

Atarah put an arm around Sarai.

"She was always very difficult every day of her life, as you know, aunt Sarai. She insisted on living in Sodom and living life her way. When our father forced her to leave with us as the city was catching fire, she fought him all the way, and then turned back and ran toward Sodom as it was blowing up into the sky. She disappeared into the smoke and gasses and he could not reach her. We created a monument to her out of a pillar of salt along the sea."

The young women in the camp began gathering around Sarai and begged her to tell them again about Pharaoh's harem and all of her adventures. She regaled them with stories of the abduction and the reward paid to Abram.

"The soldiers came in and swept us away to Pharaoh's palace. The place was enormous with golden furnishings everywhere and fluttering pale colored silks hanging from the ceilings to the floors. Pharaoh was tall and golden from the top of his crown to the sandals on his feet. We were frightened and amazed at the same time. We had never seen such grandeur anywhere in our world!"

"Oh, how amazing! And what about the harem, mother Sarai?" All eyes were wide with excitement.

"I was treated like royalty and lived in lush quarters with the other women of the harem. I had beautiful clothes. I was bathed and served by servant girls and I spent day after day in the beautiful gardens. Otherwise I was ignored. Pharaoh immediately forgot about me and never came to see me. Every day I was sure Abram would come for me, but now I know he could not. His people were no match for Pharaoh's army and guards."

"But then you all got rich! Is that right?"

"I learned much later after my release that Abram was given wagon loads of riches in payment. I seemed to have been worth a fortune! It is a good thing I did not know that immediately or I would have thought that he sold me! But no, of course he would not. We were both helpless before Pharaoh and his guards, and had to trust God's promises."

"But Mother Sarai, tell us how you came to be released!"

Their excitement was growing and Sarai was a wonderful story teller with all the drama in her voice as she spoke.

"My dear ones, I did not know much about prayer to God, but I did know the Egyptians did not know that. So every morning I began to pray in a loud voice:

"Oh great Pharaoh, please release me now because I am Abram's wife and our God will send plagues upon your house if you do not take me back to him."

"And the guards heard you? What did they do?"

"Well it seems that Pharaoh's household was already having some difficulties with plagues there and all over Egypt. So when the guards told him that the plagues were coming because I was Abram's wife and we had a powerful god who would afflict Pharaoh's house, he believed it!"

They all laughed.

"Sounds like Pharaoh was not very smart! Who could believe a god could send plagues?"

Sarai laughed, too, at the thought of Pharaoh not being very smart.

"Well, he was enraged! He sent the guards to get me and take me back to Abram's camp immediately. That was only the second time I had ridden a camel and hung on tight afraid I would fall off, but I was so happy that I did not have to walk."

They all giggled.

"Pharaoh commanded that we take everything, all of our people, herds and servants, riches, everything! And leave Egypt immediately. We packed everything up and left as quickly as we could before he changed his mind."

"He let you take everything? Even the price he gave Abram for you?"

"Yes, he did. And do not be too critical of Abram. He had many challenges and did not always make the decisions that we thought best. I have forgiven him and myself for blaming him, and perhaps that is why the Lord has blessed me to give him a child, a son."

"When we settled here on the plain of Hebron, to my great surprise, I was with child. I thought I was well beyond my time of child bearing, but God's promises come true even when we do not think they will."

"You had a child?" Atarah was all smiles.

A hush grew over the group.

"A very special child, Isaac. He has been away at the markets with the sheep, but he will be here soon. He is a gift from God to Abram and me. It is the fulfillment of a promise. God always brings promises about in a right and perfect way and at the right time. Praise to the name of the God of All!"

Abram stepped into the group.

"Our names have been changed to honor God of All. No longer are we Abram and Sarai, but now Abraham and Sarah. The Breath of God has been added to each name. We will go forth as God's chosen people, carrying the message of the One God to all nations."

Sarah stood up, smiled at him and spoke to everyone, her demeanor changing from story teller to queenliness. Her voice changed as if to echo the holiness of which she spoke.

"The Breath of God is within each one of us. We hope our new names will remind all of you that you are creations of a Most High God. The power of the Holiness as in Melchizedek is also within each of you! Be joyful and thankful! Go forth and live great lives!"

# CHAPTER 26

❖⬦❖⬦❖⬦❖⬦❖⬦❖⬦❖⬦❖⬦❖⬦❖⬦❖⬦❖⬦❖⬦❖⬦❖⬦❖⬦❖⬦❖⬦❖⬦❖⬦

# MOAB

The community of Moab was growing and prospering quickly. Almost everyone who lived there had lost everything in Sodom and Gomorrah, and worked all the harder to re-establish their lives.

Hadoram, though growing older and a bit lame, came from Abram's camp to oversee the development of the valley community as he had Lot's farm. He directed the people on how to set up farming systems so their flocks and crops would flourish. They built storage places for grain to sustain the population as it grew.

Cheran set up security for the community. His battles with the gangs of Sodom had taught him many useful strategies. There were robbers who would surely attack the fledgling community. They had already gotten the attention of a few marauders in the hills and along the caravan route. He would not risk an attack that could destroy the community and take the lives of his people.

He also became the arbitrator in the community to settle any disputes that arose. There had been a few minor disagreements that were just misunderstandings, but he knew things would eventually become more complicated as the population grew. He focused on setting up laws for the community to follow to help them keep order.

The men and women were trained and ready with weapons that they kept by their sides as they worked. They planned and built a foundation of stones for a wall around the settlement and then built it higher with reinforcements on the inside. The gate in the wall could be closed and secured at night and opened in the morning.

Tubal, the banker from Sodom, came from the south traveling with a caravan that had picked him up along the route far to the south. He was delighted to hear about the new settlement in the Moab valley, and more so that it was populated by his friends who survived the destruction. He eagerly asked Cheran's permission to settle in the community and to establish a financing system to assist in trades with caravans. Cheran remembered the help he gave Asya in setting up her business and was grateful to accept Tubal's help. The family knew him to be honest and trustworthy. Tubal set to work immediately creating a bank and financing that traders would recognize and admire.

Asya and Anah were busy planning and setting up community events so the people could come together socially for meals, music, and dancing. As the caravans began to bring goods, Asya and Anah once again created a clothing line, some for local people and some to trade. They taught the other women how to help with the sewing and warehousing, much as they had done in Sodom. Their displays brightened up the valley settlement and encouraged others to be creative as well.

Anah created an enclosed child care area in the center of the village. They trained the older girls to care for children so the working mothers would have someone to care for their little ones. The older girls created toys and games for the children. Moab and Ammon loved having so many playmates and ran to the enclosure every day.

The wall was nearly complete around the settlement. Cisterns and wells were dug to insure the water supply. The population lived mostly in tents, but buildings were being erected for commercial purposes. Building homes as people desired them would come next. Older people were accustomed to and preferred their tents.

Tebah oversaw and reported to Cheran on all supplies that would sustain the community to be certain that they all were maintained at an adequate level. He kept watch over the grain, building materials, and goods. His favorite task was to insure that the animals were safe. He trained the older boys to herd, pasture, and care for them. The herding dog they found in the mountains was still with them and still eager to do its job.

The caravan that originally directed Dishon and Joktan to the valley arrived from the south and camped nearby. The leader, Adnan, recognized them and greeted them exuberantly.

"My friends! My friends! You followed our advice and came to the valley! How beautiful!"

Dishon ran to greet them in return. Joktan followed close behind. They embraced and kissed each other's cheeks.

"Come, we have young people traveling with us. Some of the elders you met have passed on, but new ones have arrived. Come and meet them all!"

They went to the caravan and sat down in the large tent together. Adnan's lovely daughters brought wine and delicacies. He introduced them as Lailah and Morah and invited them to join in. They seemed quiet and shy, and very respectful of their father.

"Have you taken wives? Do you have children now?"

"We have no wives or children, Adnan. Why do you ask?"

"My daughters are ready for marriage and I want good husbands for them. You have proven to be good men and I pray you will accept them with my blessing and a generous dowry."

Dishon and Joktan looked at each other in surprise.

"Perhaps it is time, Dishon. We have come to a place in our lives where we have accomplished much. Is this our next step, do you think?"

"We are pleased that you place your trust in us to present your daughters to us for marriage. We humbly accept and promise to treasure them as our wives."

Dishon slowly reached out his hand to Lailah. She reached out her hand to him with a shy smile. Joktan's face flushed as he looked at Morah. He was always embarrassed that he never knew quite what to say or do around young women, but Morah nodded to him and he nodded back. The two daughters then stood up and discreetly left the tent.

Adnan smiled broadly. "A wedding will be arranged for tomorrow and perhaps your people in Moab would allow us to have the celebration among them."

Dishon was still recovering from the sudden change in his future and was barely able to find his voice.

Joktan jumped in, "I am sure they will be delighted!"

"Now that is settled! Tell me what your new little city is like. Do you have a market place? Are you ready for commerce?"

"Yes! Yes and you are welcome to come in, look it over, and help us learn more. Please, my people are friendly, hardworking, and would welcome ideas from afar to enhance the goods they make. My mother, Asya, is a designer and her people make wonderful clothing you may be interested in."

"The House of Asya! Of course! I know of your mother's creations. I pray they were not destroyed in Sodom. That would be such a tragedy!"

"Not all. Much of her stock was at the farm and carried away to safety in case the farm would be destroyed. That viper, Jahdiel, was on the road near the farm and rushed to save them. He thought to keep them, but we convinced him to bring them back and any proceeds if he sold some of them."

Dishon smiled as he drew the handle of his knife from the folds of his robe to show Adnan.

"And our sister, Atarah, is very capable with the knife if he objected. He had heard of her reputation and immediately became quite cooperative."

Adnan laughed and nodded vigorously.

"Atarah is your sister! That is wonderful. Perhaps I will have the pleasure to meet her someday! Of all the merchant thieves on the road, Jahdiel was the worst. I will be happy to visit Asya. I am sure she will have many new and wonderful garments to show. Oh, yes! And she has a sister, Anah. Is she with Asya too?"

"Yes, she is," affirmed Joktan. "Please come tomorrow. We will arrange a welcome for you and your caravan people."

"We will come and we will also arrange the wedding for the evening. My people will bring all the decorations needed and the dowry."

Asya was stunned at the sudden turn of events and dropped the garment she was working on.

"You both are to be married? Tomorrow? Who are these girls and how did you meet them? Let me call Cheran! You must tell us both how this happened."

"Yes, mother, we are to be married. They are from the caravan that pointed us to this valley when we were still in the cave on the other side of the mountain. Those people were very hospitable and gave us many gifts to help us start our valley community. Adnan knows of you and the House of Asya.

"He seems to be a very good person and his daughters are lovely, if a little shy. They are precious to him and he would not entrust them to just anyone. He offered them to us because he trusts us."

Cheran sat down and tugged at his beard a bit in deep thought. Then he smiled and nodded his head.

"I am sure what you say about him is true, that he is a good man. I will go to meet Adnan now and discuss this with him. I would like to know more about him and what our future as a combined family will mean."

Cheran and Tebah went immediately to the caravan in search of Adnan. Asya waited anxiously for Cheran to return and tell her everything.

There was a flurry of activity as Asya and Anah created displays. Their garments were beautifully laid out and new silk materials were draped around them.

Adnan and his people arrived shortly after sunrise and eagerly inspected everything in the market. He was especially attentive to the beautiful Asya and her display.

Cheran appeared and stood close by, calling out to Adnan.

"Magnificent! Do you not think so?"

"Ah, yes Cheran. Magnificent indeed!"

Adnan perceived the underlying message immediately and bowed.

"Your wife is a queen among women and shall be treated accordingly, I can assure you."

"Thank you, Adnan, for your understanding. Also my guards will be on alert for anyone who might try to interrupt or attack us during the celebration. We have been safe within these walls until now, but marauders might think that during the celebration we would be vulnerable.

"Of course, my friend! And we will also keep watch. My people will be joyful and armed. We are accustomed to defending our caravans and our nomadic way of life along the highways."

Adnan's people went about setting up for the wedding ceremony. They brought canopies for shelter, magnificent cushions for comfort, and food of every variety. Both communities blended easily and worked joyfully together creating a wonderful celebration for the brides and grooms, and the joining of their families.

Dishon and Joktan were handsomely dressed in wedding garments supplied by Adnan's people, and the brides were beautifully attired and bejeweled. All four were breathless as they looked at each other for the second time. The feasting, singing and dancing went on for several days until everyone was exhausted.

The years went by quickly and all areas were functioning and expanding steadily in the Valley of Moab. Asya and Anah could see that it was perhaps a good time to return to Abram's camp with the children, Moab and Ammon.

"The children need a sense of family history and relatives in other places. They will grow up quickly and if they are anything like Hannah and Atarah, they be gone soon enough."

Cheran completely agreed. "When Adnan's caravan comes through this year, I will discuss with Adnan to take everyone as far as Jericho."

When Adnan's caravan came up from the south, he was delighted to escort Dishon and Joktan, his son-in-law's, his daughters, and his new relatives, getting to know them, while keeping them all safe. Cheran sent a few guards from the valley along to accompany the family from Jericho to Abram's settlement.

Laila and Morah were delighted to take care of Moab and Ammon, and got along well with Asya and Anah. Any doubts they had began to fade away as they all spent more time together.

"I guess I never considered that my sons would marry. They were always so focused on all they were doing together. They were always on adventures over the mountains and discovering new places. They never spoke of an interest in women."

Anah smiled and turned from her work to Asya.

"Should we be any more shocked at them than we are at our daughters who are so amazingly like them?"

Atarah and Hannah had found a home with Abram and Sarai. Life on the Plain of Hebron was also expanding and there was much for them to do.

The news that Atarah's brothers had married was a surprise to her, but not unwelcome.

"They can be married and have many children. That is good! I am just happy it is not me!"

"Or me!" piped in Hannah. "It will be fun to meet them. I have never seen your brothers with girls or women. It is hard to imagine!"

Asya and Anah were eager to see Abraham and Sarah again. Sarah's son, Isaac, was happy to welcome more of his family. He was much older than Moab and Ammon, but enjoyed entertaining them. It was as if they had always been together.

Sarah was delighted at their laughter and playfulness.

"Isaac, being our only child, was lonely for some cousins, aunts, and uncles. Now they were all coming at once. I am so happy!"

Sarah, Abraham, Asya, and Anah sat down together to discuss what the future might hold.

"Uncle Abraham, what exactly were God's promises? Are they already fulfilled? Is there more we should know and do?"

"My dear ones, God's promises go on forever and we are part of the fulfillment of them. Each one of you is part of that promise as you carry your lives forward."

Anah was more confident to engage in the conversations these days, and her heart was bursting with questions.

"And what might we do to carry the promise forward? If we are all part of the promise, surely God is not finished and our lives must still continue day to day. What do you believe we should do next?"

With great affection Sarah reach out and took Anah's hand.

"You must carry on your lives in the best way possible, as you always have. That is exactly what you all must do. You do not have to turn into something other than who you are.

"God made you all just as you are and is pleased with you every day. You are God's hands and feet, and God's heart. God of All continues in His creation in you and your own individual ways."

# CHAPTER 27

≈≈≈≈≈≈≈≈≈≈≈≈≈≈≈≈≈≈≈≈≈≈≈≈≈≈≈≈≈≈≈≈≈≈≈≈≈≈≈

# THE VISION

Into the midst of the gathering came a wonderful surprise, Melchizedek, the King of Salem. He and his holy priests appeared among them unannounced. Their presence always seemed other worldly.

"Peace be with you. We are here to bless the Plain of Hebron and the Valley of Moab, and to prophesy great things to come," announced one of the priests.

Melchizedek stepped forward arms raised.

"The Plain of Hebron and the Valley of Moab carry the future in its people and are the foundation for all that is to come."

The group became very quiet, even awe struck as they listened intently.

"A woman of Moab and a woman of Bethel will come together to begin a new order. The woman of Moab will join in marriage with a cousin of the woman from Bethel. Out of this marriage will come a son who will begin the great march of humanity to join with the God of All in the cosmic plan."

Asya gasped and looked around.

"Who woman could this be?"

"She is not yet born, my dear Asya. You are her ancestor. You are helping to build the foundations of this tribe of Moab that will continue bringing great people to build the future."

"And the woman of Bethel?" Anah was breathless.

"She comes from the nation promised to Abraham. The woman of Moab will be her kin and they are brought together by the great power of love."

Mystified, Asya looked around at their great gathering and for the first time felt the presence of God of All, personified in Melchizedek and each of them as one people in the great movement of humanity. The air seemed to shimmer and light was all around as Melchizedek continued.

"There will be a great king in their future. He will be revered as representing that love in expression. There will be large populations spread over the land building great cities, and many wars and many blessings as well."

Anah was puzzled. Her experience of war and captivity did not seem to fit into the great nation promised to Abraham.

"Why must there be wars? The great invasion is behind us. Will we not be able to continue in peace, building for the generations to come?"

Melchizedek seemed to smile and also look saddened.

"My dear Anah, you have spoken well. But just as your new world in Moab was born out of the destructions, so there will be other worlds born of wars and disasters. Ours is to keep our eyes on what is breaking through, and not on what is breaking down. We are not to grieve over what has been lost, but to celebrate the greater good that is coming through it all."

Sarah had questions, too, and moved a bit closer to Melchizedek.

"We long for a time when peace will come and never end. Will this ever come to be? How long will this take for humanity to learn love so we can be at peace?"

"It will continue until all the generations of humanity have learned to build in peace without the error belief that the destruction of others is necessary. Destruction is born of fear. Fear must be dissolved by love.

"Out of it all will come the Great One after the order of Melchizedek, a simple teacher, who will walk the land teaching and healing.

"His teaching will cause fear and hatred to disappear from the hearts and minds of the people who follow him, and love will gather them as one as the great nation. God of All is only Love and All Good. When humanity embodies that great love, it will experience the Cosmic Love that exists forever and ever."

Dishon was eager to begin the building of this great nation, but it all seemed so far off. He wanted to charge forward right now, but to where and to what?

"How will we, as the foundation of all this, participate in that great nation so far into the future?"

"By asking the question, Dishon, you are already in the future as here. Your physical body was born and will die, for it cannot be transformed eternally. It is of the earth and must return to the earth. You are a spiritual being occupying a physical body and living a physical life, but in spirit you are eternal. Do not run or rush forward, but walk in gentleness and wisdom each day, Dishon. It will all come to you and bless you throughout your days."

Melchizedek walked among them, stopping to touch and bless each one. Then gathering his priests, he closed his eyes and raised his arms once again. The air was electric. Everything seemed to shimmer with light and they were gone.

Everyone sat quietly for a long time, taking in the enormity what they had seen and heard. Dusk was turning into night and soon they began to silently drift away to their tents.

Asya and Anah were eager to return to the valley of Moab. King Bera, who had been living in Abram's camp, longed to see the valley and decided to accompany them home. Isaac did not want them to leave. Asya hugged Isaac. They both had tears in their eyes.

"You will come to visit us one day, Isaac, and return to us again many times. We will hold you in our thoughts and hearts until we are together again."

Joktan and Dishon and their wives were ready to return as well. Lailah and Morah were still reeling from all that had transpired. Nothing in their young lives had prepared them for this experience.

"We have been taught about the Jinn of the desert. They are evil! They can possess people and animals. They can be everywhere and cause people to do evil things," said Morah wide eyed and near panic.

Dishon put an arm around Morah.

"Do not be afraid, my sister. Melchizedek and his priests are not evil spirits. They are not Jinn. They will not possess anyone or do anything bad. Only good comes from them. They are emissaries of the God of All. They will bless us in their prayers always as you heard them blessing our communities."

They made their way back to the Valley of Moab and settled back into their lives there. The whole community came out to welcome them back with a celebration of music, dancing, and seemingly endless food they prepared.

As Dishon and Lailah lay together in their tent, she whispered, "Dishon, I believe that I am with child! Is this part of the blessing Melchizedek spoke of?"

"Yes, it surely is! The new nation is beginning all around us! When Adnan and his caravan come back in a few months, we can tell him that he is to be a grandfather in a new world."

And so it came to pass that Ruth the Moabite married Boaz, cousin of Naomi, of the tribe of Abraham and Sarah. Their child was Obed, father of Jesse, who became the father of King David.

And so the generations continued until the birth of Jesus of Nazareth, son of Mary and Joseph. He was said to be a priest after the order of Melchizedek and brought the message of love, peace, and joy to the world. It would take two thousand years for the world to begin letting go of its fear, and overcome it with love.

Printed in the United States
By Bookmasters